Changeling Press, LLC

ChangelingPress.com

Married to the Aliens

Ashlynn Monroe

Married to the Aliens
Ashlynn Monroe

ISBN: 978-1-60521-833-5

Publisher:
Changeling Press LLC
315 N. Centre St.
Martinsburg, WV 25404
ChangelingPress.com

Printed in the U.S.A.

Editor: Margaret Riley
Cover Artist: Karen Fox

The individual stories in this anthology have been previously released in E-Book format.

Table of Contents

Alexa (Married to the Aliens 1)
Ashlynn Monroe

Alexa's family lost everything during the technology bust that left Earth dependant on the Xerrians. Her only remaining commodity -- a rare blood antigen that makes her capable of bearing an alien child.

If she wants to save her little sister Sofia from a life of poverty, Alexa has little choice but to enter the Alien Brides program. She's offered the chance to marry a pair of wealthy aliens, who agree to pay Sofia's way into a good school and a better future.

Alexa finds herself on a trip out-of-this-world and into the bed of two very alpha males. Will they recognize just how priceless her soul is, or will she be nothing more than a sex slave?

Chapter One

Cold. The chill crept under Alexa Smith's worn coat. She tried to ignore her chattering teeth as she hurried toward the shelter. To her left, one thin man stabbed another for the sandwich he held. Alexa kept her gaze focused on the broken sidewalk and moved faster.

Very few safe places existed to protect the poor, so Alexa did all she could to help the sisters who ran Salvation Town. Wails from a hungry infant greeted Alexa as she pushed inside the drafty repurposed warehouse. Cots were set up all over the space and a centralized food preparation area housed their meager supplies.

At this rate, the community wouldn't last another week.

Since the Xerrans had first made contact with Earth in the early 20s, the alien technology they'd shared had broadened the gap between the wealthy and the impoverished. Alexa had been six when her mother had lost her job and they'd become homeless. By 2027 her mother was gone, shot by a police officer while stealing food.

Scanning the crowded shelter, Alexa found the baby's mother and took the can of stolen formula from her coat. Julia's eyes watered as she accepted the precious offering.

An emaciated woman coughed. Alexa went to her and handed her a crumpled tissue from her pocket. Susan accepted the offering and wiped blood from her lips. Susan had managed to break free of drugs, but that hadn't spared her from a short life in this unforgiving world. At least she had a comfortable place to die. But those desperate for food and shelter were straining Salvation Town's resources.

Since trade dealings with the Xerrans had begun included women of childbearing age, the federal government now further restricted the meager assistance they offered the poor. They needed young women willing to leave Earth. Families with the means to support themselves weren't willing to send their daughters away, so the government relied on hunger and poverty to bring them willing pioneers. The offer of a new life of comfort sounded fantastic -- if you were willing to leave Earth and never return.

Toward the back of the room, two teenage girls sat against the wall, whispering. Alexa had been worried about them since they'd arrived. They'd grown up in the prosperous part of the city. Now orphaned and scared, this life wasn't at all what they were accustom to.

"Hi, Tegan."

The older girl nodded.

Alexa pulled a small bag out of an inside pocket on her coat. "Hey, Beth." She handed each girl some precious candy. "You look upset."

The younger sister wouldn't look at Alexa.

Alexa crossed her arms over her chest. "What's the matter?"

Tegan sighed. "We've decided to go to the office of Intergalactic Communication and sign up to be brides."

"Oh, please don't." Alexa sat down next to the sisters. They were only a few years younger than she was, but she'd taken on the role of mother because it was easier than accepting she was just as young and helpless as they were. "If you do this there's no coming home. What if the aliens are cruel? I've seen the propaganda too, but I don't trust it."

Beth shrugged. "It's got to be better than dying on Earth. If we don't starve, we'll be murdered. There's nothing that will get us out of this slum. We all know it. The government wants us to go, they've made *that* clear."

Beth wasn't wrong. With daily visits from a "helpful" social worker who brought pamphlets and promises of a better life, it was easy to see the Intergalactic Bride program as the best option. She'd thought about it, more than once, but she couldn't leave her sister. Sofia was too young to sign up -- she wasn't sixteen yet, and even when she was old enough, Alexa didn't want to see her married so young. The idea of her little sister trapped with some creature she didn't love made Alexa want to vomit. Worse, rumors were all she had. The aliens were so secretive few people on Earth had seen them. She'd heard they had handsome, human appearances, but she'd also heard they were tentacle-waving monsters.

"I went to the donation center in town because I needed shoes." Tegan's eyes watered. "They made me give a blood sample for a pair of holey shoes." She wiped the tears on her cheeks away with the back of her hand.

"That's ridiculous," Alexa muttered. Her mouth went dry. This was a new low for her government. "I've heard they're looking for something that makes some girls more compatible with the Xerrians than others."

"I hope I have it," said Beth. "I want out of this hell."

"We all do." Alexa brushed her bangs out of Beth's eyes. "But there has to be another way. I refuse to believe that being sold like an animal is the only way to survive."

"You've always been an optimist." Tegan rolled her eyes. "It's cute, but annoying. You just have to accept that this is the way the world is now."

A draft slithered across the floor, and they all turned to look at the door. The social worker arrived, right on schedule. Alexa pushed down her anger at the man who'd been doing his damnedest to convince every single woman in Salvation Town to commit to the Intergalactic Bride program. He went over to one of the long tables and set a box down. Alexa watched him display toys, candy, and jewelry. Everyone stared at him curiously, but no one approached him.

"I have gifts for any young lady who's willing to submit her blood for testing. There is no age restriction on this." The social worker smiled, but the expression didn't reach his shifty eyes. When Sofia approached him, Alexa scrambled to her feet and grabbed her sister's arm.

"I know it's your birthday," Alexa whispered. "But the price of those gifts is too high. I don't trust this."

"I'd love that necklace." Sofia pointed at a locket with a rose gold flower in the center. "It reminds me of the one Mom always wore. What harm could a little blood do? They'll get it from us one way or another anyway."

When did my baby sister become so jaded? Sofia was probably right, but that still didn't make Alexa ready to hand over her blood. "Just stay away from him. Do you really want that?"

Her sister nodded. Unshed tears shimmered in her big brown eyes that mirrored Alexa's. She loved her sister more than her own life. "Damn it. Okay, I'll give him my blood."

"No, don't. I'll live without the necklace."

The piece looked identical to the one Alexa had pawned years ago after their mother died. She stepped forward, and the social worker's eyes widened. She sighed. "I'll give you a sample for the necklace."

With her outspoken criticism of him, Alexa didn't blame the social worker for the wary look in his eyes, but he nodded. She glanced down at Sofia and gave her a small, tight smile. "Just promise me you won't give anyone your blood."

Sofia nodded. "You don't have to do this." She grabbed Alexa's arm. "Don't."

Alexa patted her sister's hand. "It's okay." She pulled away and held her index finger out to the social worker. He scrubbed her skin with an alcohol wipe. Snapping the top off a small device, he pressed the tip against her, and she flinched as the sharp sting caught her off guard.

The ordeal was over faster than she'd anticipated. He put a small bandage on the puncture and inserted the device into a tiny electronic reader. Two beeps and he glanced up at Alexa. His brows drew together, and he shook his head before sliding the necklace in her direction. Without a word, he packed up the other items and left.

"That was weird," Tegan said as she walked over to stand next to Alexa.

"Yeah, it was." Shivering, she rubbed her arms, but the cold ran soul deep. "Really weird." She looked down at the necklace and handed it to Sofia, her lips twitching into the best attempt at a smile she could muster. "Happy birthday." She had the oddest feeling this might be the last time she ever had the chance to tell her sister those words.

* * *

Rexxon read the file on Alexa Smith for the sixth

time. She was perfect. Almost too good to be true, and her blood work matched what he needed better than any of the other girls interviewed to become theirs. The only problem was Alexa hadn't interviewed. The account of her life stated she wanted nothing to do with the Intergalactic Bride program.

He set the digital paper, a flexible device connected to the intergalactic database, and pushed his long brown hair out of his eyes. He looked forward to cutting it after *Et Lamour*, the mating. Sighing, he pinched the bridge of his nose. When he and Tavvor had made the decision to take on a female in the ancient tradition, they'd never imagined it would be so difficult.

The door to his private room opened with the subtle swish he'd grown accustomed to since they left their home world to orbit Earth.

"You've found her?" Tavvor asked. He sat down next to Rexxon's desk and picked up the digital paper. His eyes widened. "She's so young. Isn't there a more mature woman who is right for us?"

Rexxon shook his head. He reached out and tucked a strand of Tavvor's black hair behind his ear. "You still want her, right? We've come a long way to complete our lives."

Tavvor's rugged, albeit handsome, face appeared grim as his lips turned down at the corners and his brow furrowed. "The idea of holding her, our third, fills my heart until I can't speak my joy, but having to resort to bribing a scared alien child does not. Have these girls even been initiated into the ancient rite?"

Rexxon rubbed his temples. "Unfortunately, ours would be a perfect match for us, except for the fact that she doesn't even want to leave Earth. No other woman on this planet can be so right for us, but she has a sister. According to her file, everything she does is to protect the younger female. She has not entered the program. I have sent an emissary to her, but I fear she'll decline. I've given my blessing for them to offer financial compensation."

"Financial compensation? I would never want a woman who would sell herself, and neither would you."

"That's not what I meant. I have assurances she's not the type of woman who would shame our union. She's loyal, protective. I'm betting, praying actually, that she'll trade her life on Earth for her sister's future."

Tavvor nodded. "I see. She would secure the younger woman's future on Earth before making a place with us for herself. Admirable. I need to read her file, but I trust your judgment completely. If you would unite with her, then she is the one. I long to have my full power as a warrior freed. It's such a shame soul trinity is taboo. The politicians fear our power."

"That same power won the war," Rexxon said. "But I understand how terrifying it must be for a woman to give herself to two warriors who gain strength and higher awareness from orgasm. War breaks the minds of weak men."

Rexxon hung his head, unable to meet Tavvor's eyes when he remembered the brutality of the *Kaalh* sect. He folded his hands and stared at the scars on his wrists, where Tavvor's physical manacles had left marks on his own skin, more than a thousand miles away. These monsters had used the most brutal torture trying to break Tavvor because of him. If anyone should have died or come home changed it should be Tavvor, but Rexxon held a piece of his friend's mind and took on some of the torment. "After so many of our sect came home brutalized and mentally wounded, and so many women in soul trinity died, the council wanted to prevent such pain in the future. I was the only one who stood against the decision to stop soul trinity. Finding Earth was good fortune."

"What if she will not come to us?"

Rexxon grimaced. "Then we persuade her." *Alexa Smith will be ours, one way or another.*

Chapter Two

Alexa grinned. He'd come home. She'd missed him. Soul trinity wasn't enough. She needed to touch him. Rexxon leaned in and kissed her. She didn't pull away. She was starving for his kiss. He'd promised to be home a week ago, but a treaty needed signing and her beautiful Rexxon was one hell of a negotiator. She touched her rounding middle.

"My soul, I've missed you. Has Tavvor been doing his duty?" Rexxon's sexy accent was a total panty dropper. They knew English, so Alexa had given up learning the tongue of their sect years ago. Rexxon pressed his mouth to hers again, this time with more need. She smiled against his lips, and he moaned, deepening the kiss, and she opened for him to slip his tongue inside. He explored her, tasting spicy and exotic. She muttered with disappointment when he pulled away and touched her face.

"Are you feeling well? You give me -- us -- a third child soon."

"You're adorable. Seriously, we've been over this a million times. You won't hurt the baby or me."

He pulled her against him tight. His erection pressed against her hip. He stared into her eyes again. "You are the greatest treasure of my life. I would never endanger you." Rexxon ran his hand down her back. "Being inside of you makes me so powerful that I fear my strength when I hold you." He brushed her lips with his again gently, once, twice, before crushing his lips to hers in a brutal kiss that left them both panting.

He stepped away, but only far enough to pull his shirt over his head. She'd been lying in bed, naked, anticipating his arrival. Tavvor had told her Rexxon had finally returned and Tavi -- Tavvor hated it when she used the Xerra pet name on him -- had taken the children out so she and Rexxon could have some time together.

When Rexxon pulled her back into his arms, she kissed him with everything she had. Her arms wrapped around his neck and she tangled the fingers of her right hand in his hair, but her left hand slid down his chest into the thin patch of dark brown wiry hair between his nipples. She followed the trail down to his belly button. The ab muscles under her hand rippled. He wore the baggy pants of his one in his position that tied at the waist, and she tugged the belt loose. The clothing dropped to the floor.

Alexa bit her lip. His tan, lanky body fueled her lust.

Rexxon stood next to the big bed the three of them shared, and he pulled her close. "Submit to me, woman." He massaged her shoulders.

Alexa sighed with pleasure. "I'm yours. Use me until I can't think straight." Panting, she tried to slow her racing heart as she gulped down a deep breath. What was coming was good, so good. Her pussy ached.

The flash of lust in his eyes was unmistakable and her cheeks burned. The pads of his fingers brushed her nipples as he took her breasts in his hands. He stroked them until she groaned and arched into his touch. Then his fingers moved to skim her sides before his palms rubbed against her ass. He pulled her close, and his erection pressed against her belly. He ran his hands over her flat stomach before he lightly skimmed her hips. She moaned as he brushed her mound and then his thick fingers caressed her labia, parting the folds, and finding her wetness. Hot and needy, she wrapped her arms around his neck and pressed against his touch. When he gently rubbed her clit, she jerked, groaning.

Alexa reached out and took his length in her hand. He was hard, and the velvet sensation of his skin in her palm was silken steel. He was hot; even his dick was beautiful. His shaft was thick and well formed. He wasn't as long as Tavi, but he always hit the right spot, and she came hardest for him. She stroked him in a slow rhythm and pulled a growl from low in his chest. His eyes half-closed and darkened with lust. Rexxon pulled her close, fast, and kissed her. She moaned into his mouth as he controlled the kiss. His fingers tangled in her hair when he clutched her head, holding her steady. He wrenched his mouth away from hers and stared deeply into her eyes. Her breath caught in her throat. His mouth went to her right breast, and he kissed her nipple reverently before drawing it into his mouth and sucking hard.

She arched her back. "Rexxon!"

Alexa took his cock in her hand, using careful precision to grip him. He sucked in a breath and let it out with a groan that was almost a sigh. She explored his erection and sac with her fingers as he devoured her. Pleasure made her shiver as he ran his teeth over the sensitive nub. She closed her eyes and rubbed her hand faster up and down his length.

He moved to the other breast, drawing that bud between his teeth.

She cupped his sac, and Rexxon exhaled.

Alexa nipped his earlobe. "I want you right now." Her voice was strained with raw need.

He pulled away just long enough to pick her up.

"What are you doing?"

"I'm fucking you on our household alter to give thanks. The gods have given me so much. I want them to feel my joy when I come inside of you."

Rexxon looked into her eyes. "There is no going back from this. When you give yourself to me today, I want you to promise my gods you will never return to Earth. I need reassurance. I dreamed I lost you last night."

"I'm not going anywhere. Not when I'm so happy right here in your arms, in Tavi's. I love you both."

* * *

Gasping awake, Alexa sat up in bed, feeling exhilarated and violated at the same time. She looked around, but the other women still slept peacefully on their cots. Sister Margaret snored softly. Alexa flinched when she looked at the loving albeit zealous woman, superstitiously afraid the sister might sense the wickedness of the dream. Sofia rolled over, and her peaceful young face calmed Alexa's racing heart. *Everything is fine. I'm here, and I'm safe.*

Alexa finished the last of the breakfast dishes before glaring at the man entering Salvation Town. She was already grumpy from lack of sleep and no coffee. They had run out, and no one had donated any recently.

Sofia shook her head. "Sis, sneak out."

"Here he comes again," whispered Tegan.

Alexa blew the bangs out of her eyes. "There's no point in hiding. I tried. He'll just wait me out."

The man was short, for a male, and balding. His beady dark eyes reminded Alexa of a rat. The emissary for the Intergalactic Bride program had started coming around shortly after she'd given the blood sample. He gave her one of his creepy smiles, and she shivered. "Good morning, Miss Smith."

"It was," Alexa mumbled.

"Pardon?" His brow rose.

"Nothing. Hello again, Mr. Johnstone. My answer won't change. You can show up five hundred times a day, and I'm still going to tell you I've zero interest in the program. I'm an Earth girl, and that's that."

"I have something new to bring to the bargaining table today. I think you'll be pleased, very pleased."

Curiosity, her greatest weakness, got the better of her. "I'm listening."

"This would best be discussed in private. Would you be willing to sit in my car for a private discussion?"

"No way! I'm not an idiot. You'll kidnap me."

"I promise you I have no ill intentions. These young women are our witnesses. If you aren't back in thirty minutes, they can call the police."

Tegan crossed her arms over her chest. "Yeah, like the police will rush right over to help out a woman in Salvation Town."

Sofia stomped her foot. "I'm not going to let you take her."

The man shrugged. "Fine, but can we at least find a private place to chat?"

"As long as we don't leave this room, I'll talk."

They went over to where a group of long tables with benches awaited mealtime in the corner and sat down. Tegan and Sofia sat down across the room, but they kept watch. Knowing she wasn't alone with the man eased some of Alexa's anxiety, but she didn't trust anyone associated with the bride program.

Alexa frowned. "I'm listening."

"Good. I know you care deeply about your sister --"

"Don't," Alexa interrupted. "Don't you dare

bring her into this. I wish I'd never given you people that sample of my blood. I knew better, but I -- it doesn't matter. It was a mistake. You'll never get her blood, not as long as I can help it. Whatever has you so interested in me doesn't necessarily live in her too. She's never leaving Earth, never."

He raised his hands in surrender. "Please, calm down, Miss Smith. I'm not going to suggest your sister join the program. She's too young. I'm not even going to ask for a sample of her blood. What I want is you. Your future spouse would like to adopt your sister into his sect. She could stay on Earth as an honorary member of his family, giving her complete diplomatic immunity from the program, and he would pay her a monthly stipend, provide housing, and see that she has an education."

Alexa's throat closed. That was everything she'd ever wanted for Sofia. *How can I say no?*

Johnstone leaned closer. "Can you honestly tell me you're happy here? Can you tell me you've never wondered about what was up there?" He pointed at the ceiling, but she knew he meant the stars. "Your sister would be safe, and you'd be going on an adventure humans have pondered since the beginning of time. You'd know what's out there."

She swallowed, her mouth dry, and her heart racing. "I -- I need time to think about this. How would I know he kept the promises to me and provided for Sofia?"

"Here's a written contract for you to sign. Your prospective husband asks you to keep the details private, as this is not a common practice, but he will see that she has a subspace communicator so you can stay in regular contact. You won't be saying goodbye forever."

A terrible chill ran through her blood. "How does this guy even know about me, about Sofia?"

"The homeland security protocols have become very tight in the last thirty years. Your government is very careful."

"What do you mean? The government has provided the aliens with intel on Sofia and me?" Alexa bit her lip until it hurt. She was afraid she might scream in sheer frustration.

"Every female in this country is a commodity our friends from Xerra have an interest in. There are files on everyone, your sister included. If she does have the right physiology, she's valuable, but diplomatic immunity would keep her out of the program. She won't even be eligible. You'll have essentially tied her to Earth for the rest of her life."

Alexa liked the sound of that, but the price was so high. "My want-to-be alien husband knows about me, but I have nothing to base my decision on. Can I speak to him before I make my choice?"

"No. The rules are very clear. For the protection of both parties, no meetings take place until the paperwork has been finalized. These men are the most powerful and wealthy on Xerra. Strict procedures were put in place for the protection of all involved."

Alexa slumped. Her mind raced as fast as her heart. This was a big decision. *Can I leave Sofia alone, with no one, nothing but money?* Thinking of all the birthdays and Christmas mornings her sister would sit alone made Alexa a little sick, yet the assurance she'd be safe was very appealing. "I need to talk to Sofia." Johnstone started to stand, but Alexa grabbed his arm. His brows drew together, and he sat back down. "Have you met him?" Alexa hated how timid her question sounded. "This man who would take me away into the stars, have you met him?"

Johnstone shook his head. For the first time in their short acquaintance, Alexa detected no artifice in his expression. "The privacy of our clients is guarded. I've never met him, but I can tell you he's passed all of our vetting procedures and is in the most elite echelon of the program. He's a man highly regarded on his world. Coming here for you was something he would have spent a great deal of consideration and resources to accomplish. He's been waiting a long time for his selection. He picked you out of hundreds of applicants. He's seen countless videos of some of the most beautiful girls on Earth begging to be his bride, and yet he's invested considerable energy and funds to secure you. He needs you."

Alexa nodded. *Being needed isn't the same thing as being loved, but heck, it's something.* "Thanks. I'll look this over and talk to my sister. I -- I'm not sure this guy knows what he's actually buying here. If you have a way, let him know I'm stubborn as hell and I won't tolerate being abused. I'll protect myself."

"Of that, Miss Smith, I have no doubt. I have never had so much trouble convincing someone to join the program. You aren't easily swayed. Coming to see you hasn't been the highlight of my days these past few weeks, but I have developed an odd affection for you. I'll do what I can to relay your message."

"Thank you. Oh, and tell my alien husband that you can take a girl out of the Earth, but you can never take Earth out of the girl. He's getting me as I am, nothing more and nothing less. I'll be kind to him if he repays me with the same courtesy."

Johnstone nodded, started to leave, then stopped. He turned around again. "One more thing. There's something on page fifteen of that contract I want you to pay very close attention to. Something that not all contracts have. In fact, only one percent of the women leaving Earth leave for this kind of marriage. Be very sure, because that is the very reason why you're so precious to them."

"*Them?*"

"Read the contract. I will be back in two days. If you're amicable to the agreement, have your affairs in order and say your goodbyes."

"That sounds like a death sentence."

"It's not death, but it's the end of who you are today and life as you know it. We all wear hats: sister, friend, daughter, neighbor, Earthling. This hat you're going to put on is unlike any of the others you've ever worn. I'll have a witness and notary ready for your signature in case you want to sign."

Alexa couldn't breathe as she watched him walk out the door. She had some heavy reading to do. And a hard conversation to have with Sofia.

Chapter Three

Rexxon watched his closest friend pace the room.

"What kind of insult is this?" Tavvor tossed the digital paper on the desk.

Rexxon grinned. "I think it's a good sign."

"Good sign? She promises a battle."

"And would we want a timid girl to complete our souls? Seriously, I am always amazed at your lack of vision, my friend." Rexxon picked up the digital paper. He couldn't resist reading the words again.

I am pleased to report Miss Smith is reviewing your generous offer and has expressed interest in the opportunity to have her sister adopted by your royal house and given diplomatic immunity. She was grateful for your pledge to keep her sister in housing and provided for, especially your gracious offer of an education.

Miss Smith requests I humbly express her thoughts on exactly who she is, beyond the mere description you have read. She wants you to know she will always be a woman of Earth who knows her own heart and will not suffer abuse if she agrees to enter into this contract. She has expressed her wish for a harmonious home. Miss Smith has stated she would give you the same respect and kindness you provide to her.

On a personal observation, she's a very passionate and caring young lady who is not afraid to speak her mind. She will require a certain amount of understanding, possibly forgiveness, on your parts. As you know, Earth women are not accustomed to

**your traditions, and Miss Smith has had no education
in your ways or what a polyandrous marriage to your
kind would mean to her physical and emotional well
being. I would stand in for her deceased father in this
matter.**

**Sincerely,
Jonathan Johnstone**

Rexxon had never heard of any other program
emissary or ambassador reaching out with such
demands. If Rexxon had interpreted the letter the same
way Tavvor had, Jonathan Johnstone would lose his
job. Instead, Rexxon's respect for the man grew.
Johnstone understood Xerrian culture. He knew
without a male relative to speak up for her in this
ancient rite of marriage, Alexa would essentially have
handed over her rights without recourse.

Johnstone's message gave the girl a very
important security net. If she reached out to her
emissary at any time and told him she was being
abused in any way, she would have had the right to
end their bond, both spiritually and legally.

"She must be a very special woman to have
inspired this man to risk his livelihood. We both know
what a savage planet Earth is. Without a job, he and his
family could end up homeless and hungry. We made
sure he had never met Alexa Smith until he became
our emissary. I'm impressed. This act honors us."

Tavvor scowled. "How so? We would have had
the security of knowing she was ours for life if he
hadn't intervened."

"The first principle any warrior learns is that
earning the respect of the enemy becomes a powerful
weapon. They battled, and she won his respect. Alexa

Smith is a born warrior. This man has given us proof of how special she is. My heart is content. He will be honored as her father during the ceremony, and we will have it on Earth."

"What? You're joking."

"I would not joke about this. I, too, would like to honor our bride's strong will. We will give her the opportunity to marry us on her world, which also gives her the chance to run. If she is really the woman who's right for us, we will bring her home in the full knowledge that our happiness will be complete because she is willing."

Tavvor crossed his arms over his chest. "I don't like this."

Rexxon grinned. "You will. The moment she concedes our victory in bed, you will."

Tavvor frowned, but then a small grin tugged the corners of lips up. "That does sound better than bringing home a scared alien girl. I would prefer a wife who wants me."

"As would I." Rexxon rubbed his sore neck. "I need to get back to the council, and you have our businesses to run. I'm glad our patience is finally rewarded with the right woman, not just the most beautiful or cunning Earth girl Johnstone could find. I get the impression that Alexa Smith will come to us ready for one final battle. If we use more mercy than force, we will be the victors."

* * *

The contract hadn't been easy to understand, but page fifteen made one thing very clear. Alexa was agreeing to a marriage to two husbands. Alexa looked around one last time. The dingy warehouse had become home. She hugged her sister, and Sofia's tears wet Alexa's shoulder as they embraced.

"It'll be okay. We talked about this. They'll let us communicate."

"Why can't I go with you?"

"Xerra has a lot of rules. When someone from another planet goes to live there, it's called a migration and only a migrant who has married --" Alexa's throat grew dry and tight and she stopped to swallow. She hadn't told her sister about the polyandry. "One or more citizens of the planet can migrate. I'm not scared. This contract is very firm about my safety."

"But a contract isn't going to stop someone from hurting you while they're doing it." Sofia pulled back. Tears rolled down her face.

"I've called ahead and they've agreed. We'll be able to see your new home before I leave. Your happiness and success are all I've ever wanted."

"I won't let you sacrifice your life for me."

"I'm not. I've always wanted to travel. Not only will I see the stars, but I'll be able to see a whole new planet. You know I'm fascinated with what's out there. They've told us so little about their world. Now I get to see for myself. I'll be talking to you every day. You're considered an alien diplomat now. We've made it. We survived Salvation Town. Sister Anne promised to watch over you. She'll be coming by your new home every few days to make sure you're doing your school work and behaving."

Sofia covered her face with her hands. "You're going away forever. It's like you're dead."

"I'm right here. I'll be talking to you every day and watching out for you from the stars. You aren't alone. This isn't like when Mom died. I promise it won't be like that."

Sofia glanced up. "For sure?"

"Definitely."

The Salvation Town sisters came over. They all had tears in their eyes. Sister Margaret, the most pious of them, pressed a cross into Alexa's hand. Sofia hugged Sister Anne, and the nuns started blubbering goodbyes as Mr. Johnstone arrived. He wore a tuxedo. His big smile was warmer than Alexa had expected. He walked over to her and hugged her. *Awkward.* When he pulled back, his smile slipped. "I have been invited to your wedding. I'm to give the bride away, or the Xerra equivalent."

She scowled. "Why?"

"Your new husbands contacted me and said they want to give you all the respect and honor they have the ability to offer you. They are going to have the wedding on Earth instead of in space to ensure it's fully recognized legally by Earth traditions. I'm standing in as your male relative. If you ever want out, all you need to do is contact me and I'll have the right to extract you from Xerra."

"You would do that? If I call you would help me come home?"

He looked deeply into her eyes. The serious expression of contemplation on his face made her heart clench painfully. "Yes. I believe you would only reach out if you're suffering. I honestly believe, if you enter into this commitment with an open mind, everything will work out. Have you read the contract and do you understand it?"

"I asked one of the sisters for help, and she found a lawyer willing to assist me with the jargon. Yes, I understand. Page fifteen was a shocker, but I'll agree."

Johnstone rubbed his hands together. "Great. I think you're making the right choice."

"That makes one of us."

He frowned, and his gray brows drew together.

"I did relay your message, as well as I could, and this unique ceremony is the result. These men are clearly trying."

Alexa sighed and nodded. "I guess you're right." She leaned closer to Johnstone. "I -- I'm a little scared."

A kind expression blossomed on his face. "I'd be worried if you weren't. Every bride is nervous on her wedding day, but you're giving up everything you've ever known to pioneer a new life with not one, but two husbands."

Alexa looked over at Sofia and made sure she wasn't listening. Tegan and Beth had come to say goodbye. They were both hugging Sofia at the same time.

"You're doing this for a noble reason. Xerra has different sects -- think of them like city-states, but more religions than governments. The planet has one massive continent broken up by huge rivers. The Xerrians live nearly three times as long as humans, but reproduction is a much greater challenge than it is here on Earth. That's why they want our females." He paused as if letting this poorly hidden truth sink in.

"The husbands you have are from the most ancient and traditional sect. They value sacrifice, and I think you've impressed them. It's a good start." He, too, glanced over at Sofia. "I'll watch over Sofia, as well, since I've inadvertently adopted you." He chuckled. "You're leaving her with more family than you realize. She'll be fine. Now it's time for you to focus on you."

"Mr. Johnstone, I know we started off on a bad foot, but I appreciate your compassion."

"You've made an impression on me, and I believe you've done the same for your new husbands."

"Is there any way we can hide the fact this is to

be a polyandrous marriage from my sister? She's young and scared. I don't want to make this weird and confusing."

He nodded. "You should leave Sofia at her new apartment, instead of bringing her to the ceremony. You can focus on yourself instead of worrying about her. I don't believe you do that very often."

"She's kept me going. Worry has been my fuel. I'm not sure I can get through the ceremony without someone to take care of."

"What about your new husbands? Consider directing your empathy at them."

Alexa's head tilted and she squinted up at Johnstone. "Why?"

"I don't have all the details -- Xerrians are not exactly open about their culture -- but I know far more than the average Earthling. Soul trinity is something they had to travel to Earth to complete. They're desperate enough to travel across galaxies to find you. They have to be nervous too. This union is a religious experience for them, not just a legal contract."

As strange as it was, Mr. Johnstone's advice was good. This whole situation was awful, but knowing the aliens might not be overjoyed made her feel better, not worse.

The notary and witness arrived, and Alexa signed the paperwork at the same table where Mr. Johnstone had handed over the contract.

With a single flourish of a pen, Alexa signed over her life. She walked over to where her sister and friends waited. Tears flowed, and they exchanged hugs before she was hustled outside in a whirlwind of shock and into the back of a limo. Sofia waved out the window, but Alexa didn't have the energy. Her single bag sat between her feet. She stared down at everything she owned and realized she didn't even have anything nice to wear to her own wedding. That was the moment the gravity of the situation hit her, and suddenly she struggled to hold it together.

Mr. Johnstone handed her a tissue. "If you need to cry, it's best to do it now and not during the ceremony. Remember, Xerrians respect strength. Find yours. I've seen it, so I know you have it."

She nodded and put her head between her knees, trying to calm down.

Sofia burst into tears. Alexa let out a shuddering breath and sat up, moving over to her sister's seat and putting her arms around the younger girl. They were both so young, but Alexa had never allowed herself the luxury of acting her age. After a time, Sofia quieted, and they just held each other until the limo pulled up to the tall building. A door attendant rushed up to help them out of the limo. He tried to help Sofia with her bag, but out of habit, she snatched it away.

Chapter Four

"We're not in Salvation Town anymore," Alexa whispered.

Sofia relaxed her grip on the backpack.

They went inside a beautiful, guarded building. Everything was luxurious and safe. The elevator carried them up to the thirtieth floor. The hallway smelled like cinnamon and lemon, not the body odor and stale garbage scents they were accustomed to. Apartment 3031A was just a few doors down, and when Johnstone opened the door, both sisters gasped. Luxury wasn't the right word. Opulent. The apartment was amazing.

"My wife and teenage daughter went shopping, courtesy of your new family, yesterday. They finished decorating this morning. Do you like it?" Johnstone asked Alexa.

"I'm not the one who'll be living here, but I love it. Sofia, what do you think?"

Sofia burst into tears. "It's missing the most important thing!"

Johnstone appeared horrified.

"I don't have you!" Sofia grabbed her sister, sobbing.

Johnstone relaxed but frowned.

Alexa patted her sister's back. "It'll be okay. I promise. It'll be okay. Look at all the flowers. It's like a visit to the country. I love the table."

Distracted, Sofia wandered over to the kitchen table. A huge bouquet graced the center.

Turning to Johnstone, Alexa smiled. "I love this. It's beyond my best expectations. It's so warm in here. Sofia won't be sleeping on the chilly concrete tonight." Her words choked slightly. "I'm so grateful."

"This is all your husbands' doing. They were very clear with me in the correspondence that she was to have the best."

Alexa's heart swelled. "I'm still not sure about everything, but seeing this helps a lot. I think you're right about saying my goodbye here. I want the last time I hold her to have her safe and sound in this building. Knowing she has a home again is a gift."

"My wife asked me to tell you she's praying for you," Johnstone said quietly. "All of you."

Alexa shrugged. "I'm not sure what good that will do, but thank her. Tell her I appreciate the thought."

He nodded. "We need to get going."

Sofia opened the pantry. "Oh my gosh! Look at all this food." She grabbed a pudding cup, grinning. "Your favorite. Have one?"

Alexa's throat tightened painfully, and she struggled for a breath. "I wish I had time. Eat that one for me. I have to go see this through. I'll contact you later tonight on that device?" She pointed to a small beige box on the coffee table. Sofia sat down on the couch and pulled the communicator toward her.

Alexa relaxed a little. *I can call. Sofia's not alone. I'm not abandoning her.* "When it blinks blue, hit the green button on the screen to answer my call. To contact me, hit the yellow button that looks like a file and tap my name twice. Mr. Johnstone assured me on the phone yesterday that the number works."

"It does. I was able to contact the ship." Mr. Johnstone took her arm gently. "It's time to say your goodbye. We need to go."

Sofia ran to Alexa and wrapped her arms tightly around Alexa's waist. "I don't want you to go. This place is awesome, but let's just get back to Salvation

Town. This isn't home."

"This is your home now. I told you we'd make it."

"But if you aren't with me we didn't make it out together."

"We did. Please, smile, don't make this hard on me. I made my choice, and I'm going through with it. I can deal with anything if I can picture you standing here in this pretty new apartment smiling."

Sofia stood up and followed them to the door. They stepped out into the hall and Alexa hugged Sofia tight. This hug had to last a lifetime. When Alexa found the discipline to let go, Sofia wiped her face with the back of her hand and smiled the saddest smile Alexa had ever seen. Johnstone gave Sofia a tissue.

Alexa refused to let her unshed tears fall. Her sister's image blurred. "You're within walking distance of your new school. I expect a full report about which boys are the cutest on Monday night." Sofia chuckled. Alexa let go of the breath she'd been holding. "Better. I love you, little sister."

"I love you too. So much. Don't do this!" Sofia pushed Alexa back and ran into the apartment. She rushed into the big pink bedroom, so beautifully decorated, and slammed the door. Alexa took a step toward the room, but Johnstone grabbed her hand.

His troubled expression didn't ease her worry. "We need to go. I'll bring my wife around tonight. We'll make sure she eats something and has someone to talk with about what you've had to do."

Alexa nodded. "Thank you. I just wish I wasn't leaving her so upset."

"When she's more mature she'll understand. We need to go now if we want to be on time."

"It would be very like me to be late to my own

wedding. Am I doing the right thing?"

Johnstone said nothing as he turned to go. Alexa gave her sister's closed door a final look. She kissed the tips of her fingers and held them out toward where Sofia had fled to mourn. "I love you, little sister."

* * *

Rexxon stood in the center of the temple, his palms sweating. Tavvor paced like a wild cat caught in a cage. *Perhaps our bride has changed her mind?* He didn't voice his worry. Tavvor was already agitated enough.

"What if she doesn't come?" Tavvor asked, not suffering the same need to protect Rexxon, as usual.

Rexxon grinned over Tavvor, but then the expression faltered when he imagined failure. "She will." Rexxon wasn't confident, but he did his best to hide his apprehension. "We've waited too long for her. The gods would never be so cruel."

"The gods have allowed our people to shun our sect, the sect that kept them safe for millennia and won the Great War."

"Everything has a season. Persecution ends, people evolve. With our third, we have the hope of truest fulfillment. We talked of this life during the war. When I thought I'd die, our bond and the hope for total enlightenment saved my life. Just because politicians think banning what made us strong will prevent future conflict doesn't mean people won't see the truth."

Tavvor grimaced. "The truth? The truth is they want warriors to go extinct so the government can do anything it likes. Earth a great example because corruption has made slaves of humans. Earth has no warrior sect, only men with the bravery to take on the role of protector. It's not the same thing. They don't have anything but the courage to fight for what's right. I respect that, but it's not what I want for our people."

"I know." Rexxon ran his hand through his hair. "That's the future of our world if others like us don't act. We have the resources to find our third, but not all warriors do. We have to tread carefully. Some have come and found asylum on Earth and look for a third in the ancient way. We've found the loophole and can marry, but eventually, the council will make laws to steal that last access to soul trinity."

Tavvor frowned. "That day we will fight."

"But not today. Today we bond with the one woman who can make us better men."

The comm on his wrist beeped. Rexxon hit the accept icon. "Open channel."

"My prince, your bride and her father have arrived."

"Excellent. See her to the ladies for preparation. We will remain here to await her. Send in Johnstone."

"Yes, my prince, immediately." The comm closed.

Rexxon turned off the device. "Anything you need to do before the ceremony?"

Tavvor shrugged. "No. You and I have been preparing for this since we were young men. It's been a long one hundred and fifteen years."

Tavvor's honesty is always what I need. Rexxon chuckled. "That it has, brother, that it has."

Alexa stood helplessly terrified as a tall man with striking almond-shaped violet eyes took Mr. Johnson's arm and led him away. Johnstone glanced back over his shoulder. "It will be all right. This is normal."

All she could do was take his word for it as three young, beautiful women surrounded her. The hotties were model tall and dressed like Roman goddesses. They giggled. *Johnstone should have mentioned this was a costume party.*

Alexa frowned. "Um, hi? What's going on?"

They kept giggling, and none of them responded. One of them whispered to another, and it sounded like gibberish.

"Do you speak English?" They were human women, but they all had an exotic look, Mediterranean or something. They were so gorgeous they made Alexa a little self-conscious.

No response, but they ushered her into a room filled with oddities. Jars that smelled floral filled with creams sat on a table. Colorful powders sparkled as the light caught the boxes they rested in at angles. The powders lay next to big brushes with ornate handles. The room was lavish. The peaceful, neutral tones and light blues were lovely. Everything smelled amazing. A garden tub took up an entire corner of the room, and it was full of water and bubbles. One of the women started to unbutton Alexa's fly on her jeans, and she slapped the woman's hand. Her new foreign friends all laughed, but she found nothing funny about the situation.

"Hey, I can take off my own pants, lady!"

They were all smiling and looking at her as if she were an idiot. Another of the women grabbed her while fly-girl unbuttoned her pants. Alexa struggled, but these hot chicks were some kind of weight lifting champions back home because the one holding her had supernatural strength. She kicked out, and the third one knelt down and held her feet firmly to the floor as fly-girl pushed the denim off her hips.

"Hey now, stop it! If you want me to get undressed, just leave the room!"

They didn't seem to care about her protests, and the beauty queen weight lifters had her naked in minutes. She stood shivering and crossed her arms over her chest. The women talked among themselves as if she weren't even in the room. Her curiosity about them was suffocating. "Do any of you speak English? Where are you from?"

No response. These girls were either playing her or she was just stuck having to deal with the language barrier. Fly-girl pointed to the water and made a small noise. She rolled her eyes at Alexa, stepped closer to the tub, and pointed again making the same sound.

"Do you want me to get in?"

The strong one all but picked her up and deposited her in the bubble bath. She splashed and fought. When the others started to help strong-girl, she just gave up and let the maniacs wash her. Humiliated and unhappy she stood with her arms crossed. One of them began to shave her legs. She held still to protect her skin from a nick, but the cold and stress made her shiver.

Strong-girl dumped water over her head, and she shrieked. Someone pounded on the door. The one who'd held her feet down ran over, and gibberish exchanged between the girl, and whoever was at the door. She returned and chattered at the other women who all giggled.

Alexa gave them the finger, and they gave her a perplexed look. "I wish that translated, ladies, I do. Just get this over with as fast as you can." She took a firm stance in the tub and crossed her arms over her chest, glaring at her nemeses. They seemed to understand because they hurried to scrub her hair and finish washing her.

* * *

Rexxon frowned. His most trusted guard had just come from the women. Alexa was not cooperating. He turned to Johnstone. "She agreed?"

The man turned pale, then flushed, and then paled again. "Y -- yes. She agreed and signed. She seemed content."

"Why is she fighting the maidens we have brought with us to see to her needs?"

Johnstone rubbed the back of his neck. "Well, it's not customary here to have maidens. She's used to doing everything for herself, others even. Servants haven't been part of her life. Do your maidens speak English?"

Tavvor exchanged a look with Rexxon and Rexxon flinched. "We didn't consider this an issue. The women in your program have learned the basics of our language as part of the program."

"Alexa hasn't been taught anything, nothing about the ceremony or your language. There wasn't time. You requested this process expedited."

Rexxon nodded. "We did. The moment I had her file, I wanted to act. Could you speak with her?"

"Certainly. I'm sorry I never thought to ask you about your staff -- uhh, maidens -- and what they were expecting."

The man stood, and Rexxon watched him leave. When he was gone, Tavvor laughed. "And so, the battle begins."

"I feel like a fool. What must the woman think?" Rexxon rubbed the bridge of his nose. The room was perfect. Too bad they hadn't planned her arrival in such meticulous detail. Tall pillars of ancient marble, imported from the heart of Xerraian mines, held the high ceiling in place. The altar had offerings of food and spirits for the gods. In the center of the room was the large mat where they would make love to Alexa, together, for the first time. Flower petals lay scattered all over the mosaic floor.

"I hope the maidens weren't too rough with her. It's a good thing we use English so often, or this could be a difficult wedding night." Tavvor stopped. He frowned. "This might still be a disaster. Do we know if the girl has been with a man?"

Rexxon shook his head. "We do not, but based on the culture I am almost positive she's never been with two men. This is going to be hard for her, but the rite requires we both have her. After tonight we can negotiate what she is most comfortable with. I know we would be content sharing, but she might prefer to keep a separate room or have one of us at a time. We have much to learn about her."

Johnstone returned. He appeared flushed and his hair was ruffled. Rexxon was afraid to ask the man for details.

"She's," Johnstone started to talk but had to gulp down a breath. "She's ready. As ready as she'll allow. The women came to an agreement, but your maidens are amused with your warrior lady and the one called Melaasani asked me to tell you that if she weren't your sister she'd expect to be thanked with jewels."

Rexxon frowned. "Melaasani has sanctuary in my home, or she'd have been forced to marry outside the sect for political motivations of the council. I think she'll survive this favor."

Johnstone nodded. "Your culture is fascinating. Earth has some quirks of culture too. Would you care for a little advice from a man who has been married to the same Earth woman for twenty years?"

Tavvor grinned and slapped the man on the back. "You people forget how long we live."

"Well," Johnstone began. "We don't live that long so twenty years is still impressive here. I would remember that a happy wife equals a happy life. If you keep a smile on her face, she'll make everything sunny in your home. If she's frowning, give her space."

Rexxon rubbed his chin. "We have a similar saying. Yes, females are the same in any galaxy. I will do my best to keep her happy, but Tavvor might be a bit more of a challenge."

Tavvor chuckled. "I think I will be able to keep her just as happy as you, my friend."

A knock on the door stole the levity in the room. All three men stood. The double doors in the temple opened, and Alexa stepped inside. Her light blue toga flowed around her, and a large golden broach pinned the fabric at her shoulder. Her dark hair sat piled on top of her head in a riot of curls. She shimmered with powder, but otherwise she had no makeup on her face.

Her natural beauty made Rexxon immediately hard. Her naked silhouette underneath the thin fabric was incredible. Her body was thin, almost too thin, but she still had the swell of small breasts. He'd seen her picture, but having her here in the flesh was exhilarating. That diminutive bit of biology that made her perfect was nothing compared to the way her eyes widened, and her mauve lips parted when she looked at him.

Alexa's eyes narrowed. "You?" she whispered in a breathy voice. Her accent was charming. "I dreamed you?"

"Yes," Rexxon admitted. "I sent you a piece of what we could have. I prayed my hopes to you."

She stiffened. "You didn't have the right to tamper with my mind." Her breasts heaved with the deep breath she took. Anger colored her face, and her brows drew together in a scowl.

"I told you not to," Tavvor said in a light tone. "Forgive the zealous fool. Rexxon is the son of our king and forgets we mere mortals enjoy our freedom."

She turned to look at Tavvor. Her brow rose. "You weren't in the dream, but you did something nice. Are you a sweet guy, or a jerk? I called you Tavi."

That drew a surprised snort of laughter out of Tavvor. His expression was a dance of wonder and amusement. "A bit of both and for the love of the gods don't call me Tavi."

That made her smile. Rexxon fought the flash of jealousy. She'd gifted Tavvor with her first smile, but he'd see it wasn't the last she had for them. The next would belong to him. "Forgive me," Rexxon said, bowing. He glanced up at her. She wore a skeptical visage.

Chapter Five

Alexa's eyes narrowed. *Son of the king. Crap, he is important? Unless they have a king of pop or a king of the hill or -- hell, I hope he isn't some kind of prince.* Both men were sexy as hell. They were dressed in the loose pants that tied at the waist, just as Rexxon had worn in the dream, and nothing else.

Rexxon's eyes were a piercing blue, the bluest eyes she'd ever seen. During his mind tampering, his brown hair had been short, but now it was long and wavy. He belonged in a shampoo commercial. Tavi -- Tavvor -- his raven black hair was long, too, and his eyes were so green they almost glowed. These men were beautiful. Ridiculously perfect. The muscular arms and chest were tan and sinewy. *Seriously, this must be some elaborate prank. Guys this hot shouldn't have to travel across the galaxy to get laid.*

Johnstone stood and rushed over to her. He offered her his arm. She took it with only a moment of hesitation. "I offer this woman to these warriors. I give her to them so that she might always be protected and her love will nourish them so that they might own the strength to protect our sect and all sects from this day forward."

Johnstone gave a polished recitation. *I wonder how many times he had to practice not to resort to reading it off his hand?*

"I bear witness," said a deep voice to her left.

Alexa squeaked with surprise and turned to see an older man sitting down in a chair. She hadn't noticed him in the room. When she turned, both Tavvor and Rexxon were grinning. They didn't look upset by her outburst, but the heat of a flush warmed her cheeks.

"Today my soul will unite with yours. Tavvor's soul will unite with yours. You will feel our needs, our fears, and you will be the cornerstone of the life we build. Do you have the courage to become part of our soul trinity?"

What do I say? No one gave me a script. Shit! She bit her lip. "Sure," Alexa said hesitantly.

The aliens exchanged glances but Rexxon grimaced before clearing his throat. "Alexa Smith has agreed to the union of souls. Tonight, in the great temple, we bind her to our hearts with our bodies. If any would stop this occurrence, they must act before the bell tolls."

Irrational laughter bubbled up inside of her and the oldies song by Metallica, "For Whom The Bell Tolls" began earworm replay in her brain. The men looked at her, but she couldn't stop the nervous giggles from making her feel like the biggest dork in the history of dorkdom.

And the bell tolled. Both men picked up matching skinny silver knives, gathered their long hair, and cut it off. They put their locks on the silver tray that stood between them where they'd found daggers.

And I thought things weren't going to get weirder.

No one had crashed the wedding to save her ass. Her ass now belonged to these hot alien hunks and her life was over. The urge to cry and the desire to laugh fought for supremacy and she stood trying to keep all her feelings bottled and hidden as her face contorted in an expression she imaged must look painfully constipated, which only made her want to laugh harder. *Not good. I'm cracking up. I'm losing it.*

Then Johnstone's words came to her as she noticed how tragic the men appeared. This was a big deal to them, and she was totally acting like a jerk.

Remorse and resentment coursed through her in equal measures as she tried to get her erratic emotions under control.

"I'm so scared. Forgive me," she whispered.

Some of the tightness left Rexxon's face, and he stepped forward and took her hand. "So are we."

Those words broke her, a little, deep inside, and she realized she wanted to make him feel better, both of them. "Help me make this easier for you."

His eyes widened, and his nostrils flared. "You just did." He gave her a small smile and squeezed her fingers.

"So, three kids, huh. I'm thinking one."

His smile widened. "And so the battle begins, warrioress."

Tavvor chuckled. "I'm more of a lover than a fighter."

And we are back to terror. She physically felt the color drain from her face as a cold chill coursed through her. Rexxon gave Tavvor an angry glare.

Alexa took a breath. *Pull it together. You knew what was going to happen, kind of, you knew.* "Sorry, this is all a bit much, but I'm still here."

Rexxon cupped her cheek. "You are." He looked at Johnstone and the elderly witness. "No one has stood against our soul trinity, and so we claim her. I claim Alexa Smith."

Tavvor stood. "I, too, claim Alexa Smith."

Rexxon picked up a cup and took a drink. He handed it to Tavvor, who drank deeply. The passed the chalice to Alexa. She peered at the green liquid. It smelled floral. When she drank it tasted a little sour, but she managed not to make a face. Rexxon took the cup from her and set it down.

The witness and Johnstone came over and kissed

her on the cheeks before they left. The doors clattered together, and she was alone with the men she'd just married. *Oh my God, I don't even know if I'm married. Is it over? Do I ask?*

"Welcome to our lives, wife. We will protect and cherish you," Tavvor said softly as he took her free hand. Both the men held a hand, and she had no idea what to do. She'd searched the Internet for details about a Xerra polyandrous marriage, but even Google was mystified.

Alexa's cheeks burned. "I've never been with two men at the same time. How does this work?"

Rexxon put his hand on her shoulder and started to massage her neck. "We take turns finding every spot on your body that brings you pleasure. We take it moment by moment, letting sensation lead us all to release, again and again." Tavvor started to rub her back. With both of them touching her she couldn't think straight.

Alexa bit her lip. *I should be horrified*. She had never imagined she would be intrigued by something like what Rexxon described.

Tavvor grinned. "Are you excited, sweet Alexa? Eager?"

Hating herself for it, she felt raw and bare. Emotional vulnerability made her uncomfortable. Still, she gave Tavvor an honest answer. "Yes. I'm curious about what this will be like. I'm not -- experienced -- I've never had sex, and I've never talked about sex. I've been raised by nuns, and in my culture, good girls don't like sex."

Rexxon made a noise that was almost a growl deep in his throat. "I promise you that there is no shame in making love to us. We will strive to ensure you *like* sex. Before the sun rises, you will like it very much."

Tavvor laughed. "I like it. My cock is aching from just talking to you, but I want to do more than talk. I want to take off your clothing. May I?"

"I -- do you have to?" Alexa's face burned.

Rexxon glared at Tavvor again. "Not yet, not if you aren't ready. Would it be easier if Tavvor or I went first, undressing?"

Her mouth was dry. The dream replayed like a porno in her brain. She'd liked what he did to her, but a dream and reality were two different things. Her courage was tenuous at best. "I'd rather not be the first one to get naked."

Both men gazed at her, and the heat of their lust made her pussy tighten. She was experiencing things she'd never imagined.

Tavvor untied the drawstring on his pants, and they were off so fast she didn't even have time to process that she was going to see a naked man. All the breath in her lungs expelled in a whoosh. His cock was long, narrow, and erect.

Rexxon waited a moment; she could tell he was gauging her reaction by the way he studied her face. Then he pulled the string, keeping his pants around his hips. The fabric whispered to the floor. Rexxon's cock was exactly as she'd glimpsed his member in her mind. *Will this feel as good as the dream? Will he hit that spot?* Alexa didn't trust her knees to hold her up anymore.

Shaking, she let Tavvor take her in his arms as her legs gave out. He carried her to the mat in the center of the room and laid her down.

Tavvor knelt next to her. "Open for us."

Rexxon lay down on the other side of her.

She glanced between the men. She was completely naked under the toga. If she spread her legs, they'd see all over her. *Not that this toga is hiding much.* She took a deep breath and found the courage to obey his request. She parted her knees.

Tavvor touched her mound gently. Alexa sucked in a shocked breath between her teeth. His fingers lingered, unmoving until she relaxed. Then he brushed her curls as he moved, caressing her labia lips. She jerked but didn't ask him to stop. He worked a finger between the folds, and, using her natural lubrication, he rubbed small circles on her clit. Tavvor seemed content to caress her as she lay on the thick mat in the middle of the room.

"Relax and enjoy the way this feels," Tavvor said.

The nub was so sensitive just from his gentle touch she built toward something indefinable.

Tavvor's soft, accented voice encouraged her. "Come for me, Alexa. Please, I want to hear it."

Tavvor kept rubbing, and after only a few moments, her soft mews of pleasure became a full-blown moan. Rexxon sucked her nipple through the material of her toga, drawing it hard into his mouth.

"Oh! Yes! Oh!" She closed her eyes and her mind went blank as sensation exploded inside of her. She lay panting, embarrassed by how fast they'd mastered her body. She'd learned the basics, and that wasn't all there was to sex, but his hand had made her feel great. She didn't have the courage to open her eyes and look at them. *I just wish my boldness hadn't gone into hiding.*

Rexxon leaned over her, kissing her. When his lips claimed hers, it was as though he seared her with fire. Her arms twined around his neck unconsciously, and his massiveness made her feel diminutive. This dominating male demanded her uncensored response, and she kissed him back as if he were the air she breathed.

Rexxon groaned against her mouth, sending a quiver through her. This virile male's response to her kiss thrilled her, and she found the courage to open her eyes. Tavvor watched them, a pleased smile on his handsome face. And his expression added to her euphoria until she trembled in Rexxon's arms.

He pulled back and smoothed the hair away from her face. "I won't hurt you."

He's misreading me. "I know. I'm not scared." Alexa gazed into his electric blue eyes and had to look away. "You -- you're both just -- this is..." Alexa couldn't find the words. She licked her dry lips. Anxiety made her teeth chatter.

Rexxon brushed his lips lightly over hers. "Yes. And you are doing beautifully. Never fear telling us what you need. We want to provide your soul the same sustenance you give us."

He brought his lips down to meet hers, and she melted in his arms. His subtle, spicy scent infused the moment, and she moaned against him. Nothing mattered but his kiss. Instinct roared to life, and she twined her tongue with his as his arms tightened around her.

When Rexxon pulled back to look at her, his eyes were darker. Alexa didn't understand what he meant by sustenance. Warmth burned in her cheeks making her painfully aware of how innocent she was. She pressed her lips together, afraid to speak.

Rexxon grinned. "When you wake tomorrow, reborn in our love, your thanks will be much greater." His lips found hers again and danced over them for a moment before he straightened and cupped her cheek. Alexa looked into his eyes until Tavvor's lips claimed hers and his intense energy escalated her desire.

Rexxon touched her face tenderly before trailing his big fingers down her collarbone. When she snuck a look at Rexxon's face, she shivered at the absolute determination she saw there. Her heart leaped when she realized how completely he wanted to pleasure her. Strangely at peace, the safety of their embrace surrounding her, she imagined she glowed warm from the inside out as these men focused completely on her.

"Before the dawn, I'll hear you scream that I own you." Rexxon moved so quickly she had no time to think as he pinned her hands above her head. She lay trapped on the mat, and her heart thundered in her ears.

Turning her head, she saw Tavvor beside her. He ran his hands softly down her torso, staring at her as if she was the most amazing thing he'd ever seen. She could feel a blush rising up her neck.

Tavvor pulled back to gaze at her while his fingers skimmed her mound. "Your body is perfect. I want to feel your softness under my hands as I stroke you. I want to smell your pussy as you grow hot for me. I like a woman to be a woman, and you are beautiful."

Her heartbeat sped up at those words. She gulped in a breath, suffocating under the sensual overload.

Rexxon chuckled. He kissed her shoulder. "I like strong women who are willing to let go and be submissive," he said softly. "Not women who are *always* submissive. You're so brave, allowing me -- us -- to teach you and help you discover your body."

Tavvor moved his hand up her side. Alexa hissed as his touch tickled. He cupped her breast. "I can't wait to watch Rexxon fuck you. I want you to want me, but I need you to love him. I think he feels the same way about your feelings for me. Do you think you could do that for us?"

"Umm..." She frowned. Tavvor stole her ability to think clearly. *Can I love them?* Alexa looked into his unique eyes, and then to Rexxon. The answer was easier than she had ever imagined it could be. They needed her, and maybe she needed them, too. She'd spent every day just trying to survive and ensure the survival of the people she cared about. She hadn't ever taken a moment to consider what she wanted, what she survived for. They could be her purpose, and if she were very lucky, she'd be theirs. *I still have so many questions.*

"Please don't be offended, but do you and Tavvor... are you... together? Do you have sex with Tavvor, just the two of you?"

Rexxon snorted. "Is our sexuality an issue?"

"No, but I've never been with two men, and I don't know anything about what to expect. I'm afraid I might make a mistake."

"*J'ema*, you couldn't make a mistake tonight if you tried," Rexxon cradled the back of her head and turned her to face him. "We are friends, warriors in the same brotherhood. We have been close since our youth, but no, we are not lovers. We love to watch each other having sex, but we have never engaged in the act together."

He waited a moment, watching her reaction, and then continued. "When this starts, just let the sensations lead you. If something feels good, or you want more, just tell us. I can't make you come if you don't let me know what I'm doing right. The same will be true for Tavvor. Don't be scared or offended if we ask you for something. If you don't want to do it just say *no*, but don't shut us out of your heart."

She smiled shyly, feeling a small weight lift from her shoulders.

"Are you still a little nervous?" Tavvor kissed her forehead. His right hand roamed her torso and chest.

"Yes," she admitted.

"So am I," he whispered. "I've wanted soul trinity for so long and now I'm afraid I'll scare you away before you can make our lives complete."

How can just a voice make me feel so sexy?

Rexxon took her hand and placed it in the middle of his chest. His eyes seemed to glow, and the intensity of his face stole her breath away completely. "I want you to know this is not just about sex tonight. I want to wake in the morning holding you in my arms and build a life with you and Tavvor. I want to be your world, and you will be mine -- ours."

Chapter Six

Alexa didn't know what to say, so she nodded, feeling the heat of another blush filling her cheeks.

Rexxon unclipped the broach and pushed the fabric off her shoulders. Cool air surged over her nipples. Tavvor kissed her bare breasts. Exposed to their hungry eyes, Alexa fought the need to cover herself with her arms. Tavvor pulled her between them and kissed her neck. He began to massage her back and shoulders. "*J'ema*, relax," he murmured.

Rexxon knelt in front of her, positioning himself between her legs. A look of adoration filled his face. *What makes me worthy of attention like this?* He gazed up into her eyes for a moment, holding her with tender devotion. His hot, greedy mouth took her right nipple in, sucking. Her sudden gasp of pleasure resounded through the room. Tavvor's hands never left her back, and the combination of Rexxon's mouth tugging at her and the tender warmth of Tavvor's hands caressing her back made her feel sexual awareness she'd never known before.

Alexa's nervousness began fading away. Rexxon kissed his way from her nipple to her neck. He kissed where her pulse thundered. Then his mouth trailed its way to the swell of her breasts. He moved lower to suck the nipple hard, nipping before he moved to the other. He let go of her and the cool air hit her wet nipple and heightened her pleasure as he found the other. He nipped at the sensitive peak and swirled his tongue around it.

The rough, warm swipe caused her to arch her back and buck her hips involuntarily. He took his time with that one, lapping with tender affection until both were stiff, sensitive peaks. When she looked down, he was gazing at her. Alexa watched him tormenting her nipple, and excitement gathered in her pussy.

Tavvor was still working on her back and shoulders, massaging her with a skill that made her wonder if he might be a masseur. Tavvor pushed the hair off her neck, his large, long fingers kneading away the knots from the stress of her day. He wrapped an arm around her, taking the breast Rexxon had deserted in his hand, and rolled the nipple between his fingers. She cried out from the wicked blend of sensations both men evoked. The competing pressures and pleasures caused her pussy to spasm.

"I'm getting your bed -- mat -- whatever, wet," she whispered. Both men chuckled. Looking down at the men touching and kissing her, she thought she might come just from the erotic sight.

"Rexxon?" She tried to keep her ass from wiggling. Rexxon didn't respond. "Rexxon, I want you." Her voice sounded choked.

Tavvor laughed softly in her ear and began kissing her neck. He worked his way to her ear lobe where his teeth nibbled softly, causing her to gasp and shiver.

"Didn't you hear me? Please, Rexxon."

His expression grew serious. "I've wanted soul trinity for so long. I will not rush."

The men exchanged a knowing look. Rexxon spread her legs wide while Tavvor stood behind him. Both men looked at her pussy as if it would be their last meal.

Tavvor moved to lie next to her on the mat. Rexxon was still between her legs, and she knew what he was about to do. Tavvor slipped his arm around her and pulled her close. He began to kiss her face and neck. She turned to offer her lips to him. He accepted the kiss, returning her passion with his.

Rexxon slid his tongue between her parted labia lips. She gripped the mat and moaned languidly, her entire body quivering in ecstasy. Rexxon's tongue swirled slow, provocatively over the sensitive nub, increasing the speed of his strokes until he lapped wildly at her clit. Her body shook and pulsed as she gave in to the startling rush. Closing her eyes, she glorified in what Rexxon's tongue did to her needy nub as euphoria surged through her. Tavvor still held her in his arms, kissing her neck and playing with her nipples. Rexxon never stopped licking but slid two fingers inside her and pumped them frantically.

Alexa had heard other women talk about the G-spot. Now she knew what they meant. His two large fingers fucking her felt unbelievably good; she nearly cried from the wicked intrusion.

"Rexxon," Alexa wailed. "More."

Sensation built higher as he worshiped her with his tongue. Each stroke pushed her farther than she'd ever gone before. He pulled his fingers out of her.

"More!" Alexa begged.

Chuckling against her pussy, Rexxon kept pleasuring her for a moment before he stopped. She whimpered. His tongue danced across her asshole; she jerked with surprise. He chuckled and licked her again. This time she resisted the urge to wriggle away. He kissed her ass cheek before returning his attention to her needy clit. The ferocity of desperation left her panting. His rough tongue slowly loved her clit.

Alexa's hips jerked, but he held her steady and continued. His hands clasped onto her sides, and he held her as his strokes became a rapid assault of sensation. He pressed his face hard against her and the rough irritation of his stubbled face heightened her response.

When he entered her with his fingers again, his busy mouth moved faster. She cried out. He knew her better than she knew herself and he brought her to the edge of release. She shattered against his mouth, and her whimpers turned into cries. She turned her head to the side and closed her eyes tight as a keening wail of bliss tore from her.

Rexxon brought her so close to the edge, she thought she would tumble over, but something entirely different began to build within her. This response was almost painful, and the pressure intensified. He moved his mouth away, but he kept pumping his fingers, and suddenly she arched her back and closed her eyes. She dug her nails into the pad. Her mind when blank as the most wonderful feeling originated in her pussy, leaving butterflies fluttering in her stomach and excitement erupting through her entire body.

Alexa lay panting, sated. Her gaze traveled down to their raging erections. Something changed and the timid fear melted. She sat up, taking a cock in each hand, and looked up at the men. They wore similar expressions of anticipation. Alexa kissed the head of each cock, paying equal attention to both. First suckling Rexxon, she licked the underside of his cock especially slowly, and it wrung a low groan from him, before she gave the same treatment to Tavvor. She put Rexxon in her mouth and sucked him gently. He groaned. Alexa's mouth slipped off Rexxon, but she still held the base of his cock as she took Tavvor next. She slid him as far back in her throat as she could, and he shuddered.

Rexxon smiled, changing positions, so she had better access to take his cock in her mouth. His body blocked her view of Tavvor. He was so large she had to fist the base of him. She took as much of him as she could into her mouth, sucking hard against his flesh. Alexa forgot about Tavvor's voyeurism as she relished Rexxon, loving him. To her amazement, desire rekindled in her. These men made her insatiable.

Rexxon groaned. Then the only sound in the room was the men's heavy breathing and her mouth popping as she pulled back. She cupped his sac, massaging it in time with the rhythm of her mouth on his dick.

Rexxon pulled her up and took her in his arms to kiss her tenderly, deeply. When he pulled away, she looked over his shoulder and smiled at Tavvor. He grinned back and moved between her legs. She wiggled, offering him her body, arching closer to his mouth.

Tavvor chuckled as if he sensed her impatience. He kissed his way down her stomach, twirling his tongue into her belly button, causing her to gasp. Then his lips found the mound just above her pussy. He snaked his tongue toward her clit and lapped at her intimate flesh. Her hips bucked, and she whimpered. Rexxon gave her nipple a quick pinch. Tavvor sucked her clit, and she cried out. Tavvor lapped at the nub, and she pressed her thighs gently against his head. Her body wanted him to do what he was doing harder. She arched up to grind her pussy against his mouth.

She gasped. "I'm so close."

Rexxon played with her breasts. Tavvor stuck his finger inside of her and found her G-spot again. Then he added another digit, finger fucking her while he lapped hard at her clit. Alexa cried out in a primal wail as her body quivered against Tavvor's fingers.

Tavvor pumped a large, long finger inside of her

as his tongue lavished attention on her clit. His face was buried between her thighs and his tongue delved into her pussy. Need built hotter in her. Tavvor continued to work on her pussy, and she cried out into Tavvor's mouth as she came ferociously. Her screams were devoured by Rexxon's kiss as the prince fondled her breasts roughly. He cupped them and flicked her nipples with his thumbs.

Alexa's eyes closed. She felt his mouth on her left breast. His lips were cold. She shivered as Tavvor drew hard on her clit and she mewed little whimpers as the fire burned to embers.

Alexa cried out with disappointment as Tavvor stopped. He moved and took her in his arms. "You're beautiful," he raggedly breathed the words against her cheek. "You're ours."

Burning need scalded her soul, and she clung to Tavvor's embrace. He kissed her throat, and she arched her back.

The mat dipped as Rexxon moved to straddle her with his glorious, muscular body. When Tavvor let her go, she looked up at Rexxon as he loomed above her like a god ready to claim her on the altar of his pleasure. Alexa's vision hazed with lust.

Rexxon made a sound that was something between a moan and a growl. "I want to join our bodies *and* our souls." Alexa's face heated. She didn't blush or look away. The heat was coming from deep inside of her. Prickles of awareness stirred within her, and her pussy responded. She reached for him and her small fingers trailed lightly down his stubbled jaw. She put her hands on the back of his neck and pulled him down to her lips. He choked out an emotional grunt and kissed her back with a ferocity that would have scared her if she hadn't already been so lost in him.

Her mind buzzed as her pussy tingled.

Alexa gasp as the head of his cock invaded her body. His eyes widened with surprise, then pain as his cock slid into her. Rexxon stilled. Tavvor put his hands on her shoulders, and the discomfort immediately turned into pleasure. He hissed between his teeth and she glanced up to see his brow furrowed. *He took away my pain.* The moment was better because it was shared between them all. A tear leaked from the corner of her eye, and he kissed it away.

"Do not weep," Tavvor said. "Never weep."

"S-sorry. I -- it's just so special that you did that." Her constricting throat made speaking difficult, and her heart gave a painful little leap.

"You are part of my soul. I will always protect you." Tavvor placed a tender kiss on her lips. He began to rub her clit, and the tsunami of desire roared back to life. Rexxon began moving inside of her. She made eye contact with him and focused on his rugged face. She gripped him with her inner muscles and bucked wildly against him, screaming his name as their bodies collided in a sweaty dance.

Her pussy contracted instantly and she knew it wouldn't take much to come again, her sensitivity peaking. His jaw was set in a firm line, and his face was taut as he focused, but he had amazing stamina. Stroke after stroke he held back, waiting to come, and she kept crying out, shaking and gasping from the intensity until she sobbed with joy. Tavvor was there instantly, holding her, tenderly pushing the hair off her face.

"It's okay to let it out, *J'ema,*" Tavvor whispered. "Let it take you."

Rexxon's eyes were an inferno of emotion as she gazed up at him. "Give me a piece of your soul, woman, and make me whole."

Alexa couldn't stop the keening wail, a mixture of great pleasure and emotional overload. Looking up into his face and seeing those amazing blue eyes staring back at her, she knew he was as deeply affected as she was. What they shared was more than just sex, maybe it was love.

"I -- I need more," she gasped.

"Don't fight it. Relax," Rexxon said.

Moaning, she followed his orders. Her orgasm intensified until it was almost painful.

"You were made for me," he told her quietly, and then he arched his back, gasping. She opened her eyes, and he gazed down into her face as he pumped into her with demanding need. Rexxon pistoned his hips a few more times before he stiffened. She moaned as her orgasm ebbed and watched his face contort with pleasure as he spilled his hot seed deep inside her pussy. Her body squeezed him tight. She could feel the reverberations of her orgasm like an earthquake's aftershocks.

Rexxon collapsed next to her, panting, his face reflecting the wonder she felt. They just looked at each other for a moment, catching their breath.

She turned to Tavvor. "It's your turn." Scalding heat burned in her cheeks as she looked away. "I want to feel that with you too."

"I don't want to hurt you," Tavvor said the words as if he were in pain. "As much as I want you, I won't hurt you."

In that moment, she was lost. Whatever circumstance had brought them together, it didn't matter anymore. She was falling in love with both of them, and she wasn't about to let common sense stand in the way of letting him know.

"Let me take the burden of guilt away," she whispered with a wicked little grin. Unable to take another moment, Alexa pulled back and gazed into his eyes. "I need you," she said without artifice. The sensual expression, half-open eyes and parted lips, on his face turning her on again. *Just looking at him makes me hot. What are they doing to me?*

Alexa panted as Tavvor rolled her on top of him. She'd never imagined a woman could be on top before. Nervous excitement sent her heart racing. She hovered over him. He watched her, but didn't try to stop her. Alexa held the base of his shaft with one hand as she balanced with the other. Her pussy was wet and ready for him. Then he was inside of her. Tavvor groaned as she slid down him until she'd taken all of him inside. He reached up and stroked her nipples, pinching and tweaking.

Alexa rocked forward. She sat up more and Rexxon put her hand on his shoulder for support. Then she began to move. Tavvor's thumb rubbed against her clit as she rode him.

Tavvor groaned as she slid down him until she'd taken all of him inside. He took both her breasts into his hands and rolled her nipples gently between his fingers while gazing up at her face and his eyes widened as she worked herself onto him. He groaned as she began to ride his cock. His left hand stayed at her breast, but his right hand snaked down to find her clit. He rubbed her pleasure point as her tight heat slid up and down on his length. As she moved faster, he rubbed her harder.

Tavvor's hips matched the rhythm she set, and he thrust deeply as she moved on him. They united with hedonistic perfection, and when she came her passion was so blindingly intense she sobbed.

"Tavvor!"

Tavvor rolled Alexa onto her hands and knees and jerked her hips into position. He thrust back inside of her, taking her doggie style, and to her delight, the pleasure rekindled. He held her hips and took her rough -- hard. Every thrust hit her at the perfect angle. His body fit hers perfectly, and his stamina brought unshed tears that blurred her vision.

"I'm so close," Alexa said, thrashing under Tavvor.

She bucked against him when he stilled. Tavvor stayed buried to his base. When she cried out, he pulled back out until just his tip was inside of her, then he thrust again. Tavvor pumped into her harder, and another orgasm made Alexa cry out. His eyes closed. The long, purely male sound that came from him only fueled her orgasm. Alexa whimpered. Her eyes fluttered shut, and she arched her back. Tears leaked out of the corners of her eyes as she kept coming with a shudder.

"Yes. Tavvor!" Alexa saw sparks behind her lids. "Rexxon!" Something deep inside of her cracked open. At that moment, she felt them, their souls. They were one.

Her pussy clenched. Everything felt amazing.

"I love you," Tavvor whispered just before he arched his back, gasping. He roared a growl of triumph, and she felt the heat of his release.

Alexa gasped, crying out with pleasure. Soul trinity became clear. He'd said she was sustenance. *It's this love. He's nourishing my heart -- my soul.*

Tavvor jerked. "Alexa! Gods yes!" His mouth remained pressed to her throat as her muscles gripped his cock, milking the last of his pleasure before his arms came up around her, pulling her close. He lay back, taking her with him and cradling her on his chest. He kissed her face and neck while murmuring words in a language she didn't understand. A profound sense of security left her warm inside. Closing her eyes, Alexa breathed in his scent. *Their scents.*

She wrapped her arms around Tavvor's shoulders and cradled him to her. The heat of his body warmed her all the way to her soul. He held her tight, his panting breaths fanning across her shoulder as he rested his head in her cleavage.

"You make me whole," Tavvor said softly.

He moved and pulled her to him for a tender kiss. She could taste the musk of her own desire on his lips, but she didn't care.

Rexxon pulled her around to face him, and Tavvor lay on the other side, leaving her sandwiched between them. With a sigh, she listened to them breathe. Occasionally, one of them would kiss a shoulder, cheek, or arm while they lay cocooned in contented bliss together. Her eyes fluttered closed as she fell asleep.

Epilogue

Rexxon looked at Tavvor over Alexa's head. She slept peacefully, spent in their arms. Holding her was humbling. He'd never imagined soul trinity would be like this -- this good. "We have to support our brotherhood," Rexxon whispered.

Tavvor nodded. "Yes. Now that know how empty we were before Alexa we can't sit quietly while other warriors are denied this strength. I feel like I could take on an army alone. There's so much energy in me. If it weren't so hard to let go of her, I'd get up and go exercise."

"Loving our woman was workout enough for me." Rexxon chuckled. "Adrenaline is in me too. Can you imagine making love with her before a battle? And that little burning bubble of happiness I feel is her -- Alexa's sweet nature. When I feel her in me, my mind is clear. The enlightenment is starting."

"For me as well. This is amazing."

"I love her, and I'll die to protect her, but I am ready to defend our traditions when we return."

Tavvor smiled, but it was a dark smile. "As am I. Can we protect her and save soul trinity?"

Rexxon didn't have an answer, but as he looked down at their woman he knew the reward was worth the risk. "We will."

Tegan (Married to the Aliens 2)
Ashlynn Monroe

Like many Humans, Tegan and her sister Beth lost everything, including their parents, to the technology bust that left Earth dependent on the Xerrians. Alone, the sisters find there is little to look forward to on Earth beyond meager subsistence living.

Still, Tegan is shocked when Beth is told her blood contains the rare antigen that makes her capable of bearing an alien child. Although they had promised to stay together, Beth is quickly accepted for the Alien Brides program and paired with her mate before she's even finished her training.

Now Tegan has a choice: marry an alien or never see her sister again. What she doesn't realize is agreeing to the program means marrying not one, but two aliens. Is Tegan brave enough to follow her sister into life on an unknown world with two alien warriors in a galaxy far, far away?

Chapter One

"Are you fucking kidding me?" Tegan raised her voice to be heard over the noise of the old gas guzzling cars that rattled along the street while the wealthy stayed safe on the luxurious magnetic monorail trains high above the impoverished areas of the city. "I don't know if I can forgive you if you go through with this."

Beth dissolved into sobs, and her big teary-blue eyes broke Tegan's heart, but there was no way she was going to let her sister make such a huge mistake. Tegan crossed her arms over her chest to resist the urge to hug her sister. "You can't go. Not by yourself. There's no way back if you regret your decision."

A soft breeze blew warm summer air through the alley. The dry air wasn't very refreshing -- the smell of garbage turned Tegan's stomach. A couple in one of the apartments above them shouted until a male in the adjacent building screamed, "Shut up!" from his open window. A homeless man sat up from his pallet of boxes and blinked up at them before laying back down to sleep off his intoxication. The bottle of cheap alcohol he'd cradled in his slumber rolled away, empty.

Beth flipped a lock of her long black hair over her shoulder. "This is the first offer I've had. What if no one picks me, Tegan?" Her nose wrinkled and her brows drew together. "I don't want to die on the street. If we stay on Earth, we'll never have any security. With Salvation Town forced to close the door and all the nuns arrested, we're as homeless as possible. Can you honestly tell me you're happy sleeping in doorways and stairwells?"

"Well… no, but…"

"But nothing," Beth interrupted. "We have to be practical about the future. I know we promised to stay together, but I'd rather have a man who wants me than one who wants babies. You saw Haggex's picture. That ridiculously hot guy wants me to be his wife. Me. I can make it work."

Tegan fought the urge to shake her sister. They might look alike, but they couldn't have had more unique personalities. "I'm not blind," Tegan whispered. "I know he's a hunk, but that doesn't mean he's going to love you. I want to be there -- not here -- if you need me! I don't want to end up a sex slave."

Beth paled. "If I have to *sell* myself, I'd rather it be to one man who's going to give me a comfortable life with a family and a home, than to an endless line of creeps." She shook her head and her hands balled into fists. "I'd be on Earth, but still living scared and hungry on the street. Either way, my body is the only thing I have of value, and I'm ready to trade."

"How can you even think like that?" Tegan shuddered. "I love you! If you do this, I'll never see you again. If we stay together we can handle anything. Neither of us is selling our body, yet. We have enough to rent a room for an entire week and that nice old deli guy gave us each a sandwich. We'll get by."

"A sandwich and a week in a bug infested room doesn't sound like getting by to me. Are you willing to give up on the program because we haven't found men who will promise to keep us together?"

It was a good question. Tegan bit her lip and stopped her protest. Maybe Beth was right. Just because they hadn't found two men to keep them together didn't mean Beth shouldn't take advantage of the only offer they'd gotten so far.

Tegan had held on to the hope they'd find a way out without the IBP -- the Intergalactic Bride Program. There was hope, just not a lot of it. "I'm not giving up.

I just want to do this together. I want to know you're all right." Tegan bit her lip as she gazed at her sister, willing her to stay on Earth.

Beth let go of a shuddering breath. "That's where we're different. I'm not as strong as you." She sighed and looked away. "I can't wait any longer."

"I can be strong for both of us." Tegan reached out and put her hand on her sister's shoulder. "I promise I won't let you starve. I'll take care of you."

Beth smiled, but it was such a sad smile the expression made Tegan want to cry. They looked at each other for a long moment, before Beth cleared her throat. "I love you too, but I'm not going to let you take responsibility for my life. We're both adults. I just turned eighteen. You're nineteen. We're too young to die in the gutter. I am going. I start training tonight. I'm going to learn to speak like them and act like them. From what I hear there's no discrimination toward Humans on Xerra."

"And you actually believe that? Remember our friend Alexa? I talked to her little sister Sofia, and she said Alexa lives in a fortress with her husbands. She's not allowed out on her own. Alexa is happy and doesn't have any problem with her overbearing alien husbands, but Sofia is troubled by how Alexa is kept by them -- like a prisoner."

"Sofia's perspective is just that -- her opinion. Alexa has a loophole because of the kind lawyer who convinced her to accept her men, and she could come home if it's bad. She hasn't come home."

"You know how much Alexa loves her sister. Staying with the aliens provides her sister with diplomatic immunity from the program and enough money to get an education and live comfortably. If they beat Alexa three times a day, she'd still stay."

Beth shrugged. "Yeah, you're probably right, but I don't think she's unhappy. I can't back out now. It took a lot of courage to make this decision, and I'm going for it. I'm not going to live like this anymore. I want a future. I'll ask Haggex to find you a husband. They're giving me room and board. We'll have fresh food and a warm, clean place to sleep tonight. We won't be renting another gross room again. It's not like I'm leaving Earth tomorrow."

Tegan frowned. "This isn't what we agreed on. You'll leave and if I can't find a husband who will stay close to yours I'll still lose you."

"Here, take the money I made today. You'll need it more than I will." Beth tried to press a wad of bills into Tegan's hand. A siren wailed in the distance and a dog trotting through the alley howled in response.

Tegan pulled away, fighting her tears, and stormed off without another word to her sister. The last few months had been really hard. She couldn't blame Beth for giving in, but they had told the agency exactly what they wanted. She and Beth -- they'd been together since the collapse that had cost them their parents. The agency had already gone back on their promises. They had no right breaking the sisters up now.

Few people knew it, but there were some aliens who for reasons that had to do with ancient traditions shared a wife. One alien would be bad enough. There was no way Tegan would take the chance of being saddled with two. The ones Alexa married might be brawny sex gods with the most incredible bodies ever, but with Tegan's luck, she'd get some old guy with bad breath and erectile dysfunction.

"No thank you," she muttered as she turned the corner. A huge poster, proclaiming the joys of the IBP, hung pasted on the door to the motel with the pay-by-the-week rooms.

She glared at the shiny paper as she ripped it off and tossed the propaganda on the ground. "I'm so sick of this crap." Opening the door, she went inside. "I'd like to rent a room."

The clerk glanced up. His brow rose. "We're weekly, not hourly. No prostitution here."

"Good. I'm not a prostitute," she said through gritted teeth.

He shrugged. "How many occupants? How many are male?"

"One occupant, female."

The man looked her straight in the eyes. "We don't allow unmarried females."

Tegan's mouth dropped. "You did last week!"

"New management this week. We got a government grant. No unmarried females under the age of fifty allowed."

"That's discrimination." Tegan paused, waiting for the man to come to his senses.

The jerk chuckled. "Yep, and it's completely legal. Find another room or join the IBP."

She slapped her hand on the counter. "I'll die before I join the Intergalactic Bride Program!"

The man had the decency to look a little sad. "It's getting cold out. A little thing like you will never make it through a winter without any of the warming houses open. I'd consider traveling south. Winter is coming, and there's not going to be many rooms for unmarried girls like you."

"Thanks for nothing," Tegan said as sarcastically as possible. The roach motel smelled musty with a hit of pot smoke. They weren't generous with the heat anyway. She narrowed her eyes and stared at the man long enough to make him shift uncomfortably and glance away. "I hope your money is worth your soul. How can you sleep at night? Just think about all the girls you're dooming."

He shrugged. "In times like these, you have to do what you have to do." He was shuffling papers on his desk, still not making eye contact.

Tegan hefted her backpack more comfortably on her shoulders and stomped out, slamming the door as she left. She hoped the man burned in hell on a bonfire of his money. She wasn't taking his advice. This was her town, Earth was her planet, and nothing would make her leave.

* * *

Tegan grimaced at the false clear blue sky and sunshine in the waiting area. The room was a hologram of a beautiful park. This was some serious tech the IBP was using to impress prospects. She stood in the doorway and glanced back outside at the gray, cold spring drizzle that saturated everything. Shivering, Tegan pulled her thin, frayed coat tighter, shrugging her backpack straps higher on her shoulders.

Considering how long the line for enrollment was, Tegan took a moment to appreciate her sister's counselor for arranging her acceptance in the program without the usual waiting period. She had been allowed to skip the registration window and stroll past the line of ragged women waiting to hear their fate.

Beth had finished her training program in record time. Her impending marriage and matching DNA gave Tegan the option to sign up for the IBP without delay. The need to succeed burned in Tegan like a bright, angry light. She resented everything she was doing, but for her sister, she'd do it. She had no reason to stay on Earth without her sister.

Tegan sneezed. The warmth hit her, and she stopped in her tracks. She lingered under the vent and closed her eyes, glad she'd soon be warm for the first time in months. The air inside drifted over her with a hit of new construction smell, yet sweet and floral. She breathed deeply. It had been too long since she'd been inside someplace nice.

Restaurants and other businesses were fined for giving homeless girls shelter. A local coffee shop had been shut down for giving out free coffee and letting girls come in and warm up for a few hours. The motel man had been right; girls were dying every night on the street. Sadly, most of them had tried to get into the program, but had either not been a genetic match or had failed to secure a husband. Few girls stayed on the street by choice. Tegan finally gave up the day Beth tracked her down to announce she was leaving soon for Xerra.

A middle-aged woman at one of the many reception desks smiled up at Tegan as she approached, holding her orange slip of paper. The woman brightened. "Oh! You're Beth's sister. Welcome." She stood up and came around the desk, holding out her hand. "My name is Janie. I've been expecting you. Let's go on the tour."

Tegan followed Janie down a long hall. Closed office doors were on the right and pictures of beautiful albeit unnaturally colored vistas decorated the walls on the left. Xerra looked like a bad sci-fi movie. Tegan paused and stood in front of an image of a tall mountain that was awash in pink, purple, and green foliage. She could almost smell the exotic spice of Xerraian food. *Could I do it? Could I live there?*

She didn't know. Deep down she didn't know if

she could handle the truth.

"Coming?" Janie's brows drew together. "It's beautiful, isn't it? I wish I could go, but unfortunately, I'm too old for that kind of adventure."

Tegan shrugged. "Adventure is over rated."

Janie's frown deepened. "Most girls I lead this way feel differently. Are you sure you want to use that pass?"

"I do," Tegan replied. Her lips compressed as she resisted the urge to tell Janie to mind her own business.

The left corner of Janie's mouth tilted up. "Well, if you're anything like your sister, you'll do well here and quickly find your mate. I'll show you to your room. You can leave your backpack there and then it's off to the infirmary for your examination and blood work."

Tegan stopped. "Exam? No one told me about that!"

Janie rolled her eyes. "Sweetie, it's no big deal."

But it was a big deal. "What else did they forget to disclaim in this paperwork? I read it over carefully."

"I'm sure you did," Janie said in a humoring tone. "This falls under the healthy clause. The IBP only selects the healthiest young women. They won't hurt you. You'll be asked to take a shower, you get a fresh hospital gown, and then after the exam, you get your uniform. It's fast and painless. They don't even do any bloodwork since you had that when you signed the application."

"I didn't sign the application yet."

Janie's brows rose. "They must believe you're a perfect candidate. It's against policy to skip the blood work. Okay, I lied. This might hurt a little since they'll take a small blood sample. Hundreds of girls come through here every day. I promise you it's safe. Only a select few make it to the end of the program. Many who don't do find good jobs working for the IBP. Very few girls end up back on the street, but it can happen."

Tegan knew some of those girls. Hopeless and scared, many became prostitutes or died from starvation or exposure. She shivered.

"But I'm sure you won't be one of them." Janie turned a corner and stopped at the door marked BLAKE, TEGAN. Inside was a simple twin bed, a chair, and a lamp. Tegan took off her backpack and put it down, but didn't take her hand off the handle as she glanced at the doorway. Everything she owned was inside.

"It's safe here," Jaine assured her. "As are you."

"When can I see Beth?" Tegan glanced at the woman.

"She's very busy. There is a lot she needs to do to prepare for her new life."

Sighing, Tegan fought back her disappointment as she followed the older woman back out into the hallway. They went down a few more corridors before stopping at a bank of elevators.

Janie put her hand on Tegan's shoulder. "Welcome to the first day as you pioneer a new life."

Pioneer. She hadn't thought of the IBP in that respect. She worried her lip between her teeth. *Does that make me feel better, or worse?* Only time would show her the truth.

* * *

Maxxen tapped the screen to re-play the video. *Tegan Blake.* The name was so erotic. He re-read her details on the digital paper even though he'd studied the biography so many times he'd memorized the scant detail. His wife, Jakkon's wife, was the piece of his heart he thought he'd never find. Her blood showed her to be their perfect match, but the video confirmed the fact for him. Now to convince her she isn't making a mistake. He replayed the segment that worried him most.

"Treat me with respect and I will mate with you and bear your children, but I'm not some hopeless romantic. All I want is to know my sister is safe and taken care of. Don't pick me if you're looking for some kind of fairytale. I'm not." He watched her fiddle with her hair. She was their match. He was sure she was. But she was jaded. Someone off to the side was speaking to her, and he could see she didn't care for the conversation.

Maxxen shook his head. "How does one so young get so world weary?" Her big eyes flicked back to the camera as if she could see him before her gaze flicked down in a demure, embarrassed way. Her moment of endearing shyness and frankness stirred him more than he'd anticipated.

With a soft swish the door opened. Maxxen paused the video. Jakkon came in. "You've found her?"

Maxxen nodded. "I have. Watch and tell me you don't see what I do."

A single swipe began her interview from the beginning.

"Hi." She paused. Her big blue eyes were so expressive. He could see pain and fear, but also determination and a hint of hope. "My name is Tegan. Tegan Blake." She glanced off camera. "What do I say?" she whispered. There was a pause before she nodded.

"I'm supposed to tell you why I'm the girl for you. I'm not. I need you. You need a wife. But we aren't in love. I'm not going to promise to love you, because I don't know if that is even possible. Treat me with respect and I will mate with you and bear your children, but I'm not some hopeless romantic. All I want is to know my sister is safe and taken care of." She lowered her lashes, and the sad downward tilt of her head tugged at his heart. Humans had no comprehension of what could be. "I want to go to your world, but I need you to accept I'll never be able to leave mine behind. You can take the girl out of Earth, but you can never take Earth out of the girl." Tegan paused.

Maxxen grinned. That part always made him smile. Loyal. That was something he wanted in his woman. He turned to study Jakkon's expression. The big man's brows drew together, and his eyes narrowed as he watched Tegan.

"Well." Tegan sighed. "I don't know what I should tell you about myself. I don't know you. You could never know me from this short video. The most important thing I want to say is that I'm real. I'm not something you are buying. I am not a toy or a pet. I am not an idea. I. Am. Real." She shrugged, and the video stopped.

Maxxen turned to Jakkon. "There are two candidates. This one is the one I want."

"You're sure? Why this girl? She looks so young and appears -- resistant." Jakkon folded his big body into a nearby chair and studied Maxxen.

"That's a hard question, my friend. I find her sense of honesty refreshing. I've watched and rewatched the two candidates, and I am certain this is our woman."

Jakkon nodded slowly. His war-battered face etched deeply with worry lines as he sat quietly.

"Would you like to see the other female?"

Maxxen reached for the Earth device given to him by the migration representative of the IBP overseeing the processing of his and Jakkon's choice.

"I trust you," Jakkon said. "But I would like to see."

Renea Jordan appeared on the screen. The girl was stunning. Her blonde hair sat elaborately styled in the elegant way the female aristocracy on his home-world wore theirs. Her slim figure was perfect for the sheer costume of a Xerraian bride. She wore the Earth makeup, and her lips had a ruby sheen.

"Prospective husband," Renea sang in his tongue. "I humbly submit myself to your care. I trust you to protect me. To guide me. I give you the power of my family name. I give you all that I am."

Her grasp of their language -- astounding. Maxxen saw Jakkon's eyes widened at the human's use of the ancient Xerraian betrothal song. He'd felt the same shock when he'd seen the recording. It was common long ago for strangers to marry and this song was from those times. Marriage customs changed centuries ago, until the Great War. Now marriages for political alliances were the norm again. But they needed something more. They needed Soul Trinity, and one of these two women could give it to them. Both females were compatible for the physiological changes, the proof was in the blood, but only one of them would be the right choice to build a family.

Renea ended the soft song and gazed at the camera, fluttering her long glittering lashes. She smiled. "I have studied your ways for years. I am ready to be the wife you've come to bring home." She glanced down demurely, but there was an artifice in the act. This girl said all the right things, but there was a guardedness behind her eyes that troubled Maxxen.

"I have seen enough," Jakkon said. "This girl is perfect in many ways, but she's not the woman we're looking for."

Maxxen nodded. His wise friend saw it too, the falsehood in Renea's careful presentation. "I will arrange the contracts. Are you sure?"

"I am."

Maxxen gave a strong nod and stood before hurrying out of the room. There was much to do secure their bride.

Chapter Two

Tegan sat in her Xerraian history class. She kept glancing at the clock and when the instructor scowled she shrank back in her uncomfortable seat. After class, she could see Beth. Today her sister left Earth. There was a bitterness burning in her that these heartless IBP people hadn't given her the whole day to say goodbye.

The other girls in the room were attentive, but Tegan had trouble concentrating. If a prospective husband wanted to give her a history quiz before picking her, she probably didn't want to marry him anyway.

She shook her head as if the physical act could dispel the mental cobwebs. She needed to put on a better act if she wanted a chance at working for the IBP when no alien picked her. The teacher glanced her way but didn't look annoyed this time.

"What was the single biggest event in modern Xerraian history?"

Three hands shot up. "Amie?"

"When the Warrior Sect of Trinity was finished quelling the uprising against the royal family they were very popular."

The instructor nodded. "And how was that the biggest event?"

"The royal family feared the warriors would take over the country. They had the strength, finances, and public support to make that possible. Soul Trinity and marriage to a warrior was frowned upon."

"How did that affect the warriors?"

"Warriors had a hard time finding brides after a wave of engineered disease swept the continent and killed many people, mostly women. The fringe supporters of the royal family's rival were rounded up and executed for unleashing such a terrible weapon, but the damage was done."

The instructor clicked on her computer's projector and an image of the single massive continent on Xerra appeared.

"Everything is ruled by one king." The instructor clicked to the next slide, a bustling city. "This is Centera, the royal city. To Earth's standards, it is almost unbelievable, but one family holds the highest power. When you are chosen for a marriage, King Verrek becomes your king too."

The next image on the wall captured Teagan's full attention. The badlands. These were the only place where the king's long arm didn't reach.

"Well," said the teacher with a sigh. "Time's up for today. We will pick up tomorrow."

Tegan was the first one out of class. She ran toward Beth's room and didn't even stop at the cafeteria. Every second was too precious. Beth was on the main level with the other women who were already spoken for. Some of these girls would be waiting months for their husbands to arrive, and some like Beth had husbands on ships orbiting the planet. She skidded to a halt at Beth's door. The room was empty.

I can't be too late. Panic welled with suffocating anxiety as her heart hammered in her chest. Tears welled in her eyes and her knees buckled. Tegan collapsed to the floor and let the deluge of sorrow have free reign. She let herself grieve unchecked, ignoring the girls who tip-toed past her awkwardly on their way down the hall, and sobbed until her head hurt.

Tegan felt a hand on her shoulder. The touch lingered, but she was too distraught to look at who was trying to provide comfort.

"It will be okay. She's doing what she believes will make her happy," said a soft female voice.

Tegan wiped her eyes with the back of her hand and sucked in a breath, ready to tell the girl to mind her own business, when the girl held a paper out. Tegan took the slim, clear sheet from her and saw Beth's handwriting.

Sis,

I'm sorry I'm not able to say goodbye. I'm a coward.

Please believe this is the start of something better. Accept fate,

as I have. Be happy.

Love,

B.

Tegan looked up. The girl was blonde with a long braid that fell past her waist. The crystalline blue eyes gazing down at Tegan were full of pity. The girl shrugged. "I had a sister too. She died, murdered for her coat. Beth did the right thing."

"I -- I just wish it wasn't like this." Tegan let go of a shuddering breath. "Why did she have to leave me like this? She's been avoiding me since I got here."

"Sometimes it's easier to cut ties with the people you love than to keep loving them when you're losing them. Everyone has to find a way to survive. Maybe this is her way. Be happy for her and find a way to carry on."

"That's just selfish."

The pretty blonde shrugged again. "Life is selfish sometimes. If everything were fair none of us would be here. IBP gives us the chance to decide what's fair for ourselves. I've seen girls like you before. Don't end up on the street again."

"Girls like me?" Tegan's voice rose. "Whatever."

"Girls who wanted to stay on Earth. Don't let

what you want keep you from getting what you need. That attitude will kill you. I miss my sister. I just want to help you." The pretty blonde handed Tegan a tissue. "My name is Mari. I'm leaving next year. I've been matched."

"Why such a long wait? Beth only got a couple of weeks after her match."

Mari wrinkled her nose. "I have no idea. I've never spoken to the man I married on paper. Whatever the reason, I'm safe and fed. I'm happy to wait as long as I must."

Tegan wiped her eyes with the back of her hand. "So, there's a chance that even if I find a match, I might be stuck here in some kind of wedded limbo?"

"I guess you can look at it like that, or you can do what I'm doing -- making the best of things. I get one more year to watch movies and listen to music. I get one more year to stay on Earth."

One more year… without her sister. The urge to cry sucked the breath from her lungs and her heart beat painfully fast in her chest. "I -- I won't see my sister for a long time."

Mari shrugged again. "But you know she's okay, and that's what you need to concentrate on. Hold onto the good. I'm learning to take things one day at a time and to focus on what I can control, which isn't much, but it's better than nothing."

Tegan nodded, agreeing with the wisdom in Mari's words. "Thanks." She meant it. The young woman had helped her more than anyone else. "I won't forget what you've said."

"Good. Now, let's grab some food before the cafeteria closes." Mari took Tegan's arm and helped her stand. The smell of fresh bread chased away some of the darkness. For now, she'd focus on that happy scent and think about her sister living like a princess.

Tegan grabbed a tray and began filling it with cheese, bread, and fruit. Everything was always homemade and natural. The food was better than she'd ever eaten. It wasn't the mystery slop she'd eaten as a child growing up in the shelter in Salvation Town. It wasn't the cheap fast food she'd bought with her begging money. This was healthy, and it was real. This was food that told her she was valuable to the IBP and they wanted her healthy. She was a product they wanted to trade.

Sighing, Tegan put a piece of cheese on top of the bread and took a bite. Her counselor, Mrs. Baker, came rushing into the room. The woman broke into a bright smile when she spotted Tegan. Mari reached out and took Tegan's hand. Nerves caused Tegan to squeeze the other girl's fingers, tight.

"I have wonderful news," said Mrs. Baker.

Tegan doubted they'd have the same definition of wonderful, but she didn't protest.

Mrs. Baker sat down. "You've been matched."

The food sat in Tegan's stomach like a lump, and she had to take a deep breath to avoid becoming sick. "How? I'm not ready."

Mrs. Baker's smile turned into a frown. "This is a particular circumstance for an illustrious client."

Tegan bit her lip. "What makes this -- guy -- so special? And why me?"

Molting red, Mrs. Baker's face became a mask of rage as her eyes narrowed and her lips thinned. "You are being given a gift. Don't question it."

Tegan flinched. She wanted to push but realized it wasn't going to do her any good. "When do I leave?" *Please be a year, please be a year.* Trepidation over the reality of leaving the planet sent a cold shaft of fear down her spine.

"Tomorrow."

"What?" Tegan gasped and turned to Mari hoping for any help, but the girl gaped at Mrs. Baker with wide eyes. "That's too soon. I barely know anything about the culture. I don't speak the language. I haven't even tasted the food. I -- I'm not ready."

Some of the anger faded from Mrs. Baker's eyes and she reached out and put her hand on Tegan's arm. "No one is ever truly ready for such a life altering change. You are a bright girl, your sister certainly is. You'll do fine."

Tegan resisted the urge to roll her eyes. *Really? Is that the best you've got?* Motivational speaking was not Mrs. Baker's superpower. Right now she needed something tangible to take comfort in -- something specific about how she'd manage.

"Thanks," Tegan mumbled. *For nothing.*

Mrs. Baker smiled widely. Her entire presence adopted a supercilious and pleased air as she stood up, back straight and head held high. "There. All better?"

"Sure," Tegan replied flatly.

Mari giggled and fidgeted, glancing between the matron and Tegan.

"Come with me," Mrs. Baker said. "It's time for a cram course on Xerra's culture."

Right now, curling up in a ball and having an ugly, self-piteous cry sounded amazing. Studying -- not so much.

* * *

"She's not of our world, our ways. I see no need for more than the most basic of ceremonies." Maxxen crossed his arms over his chest.

Jakkon narrowed his eyes. "You would begin with disrespect? You would bind her to you -- for eternity -- without the benefit of preparation."

Scowling, Maxxen considered his friend's council. *Is skipping a tedious ceremony for a culture she doesn't identify with disrespectful?* "Hmm. Will the girl even notice?"

"They teach the females things there, preparatory basics. The small amount of information we have given them is imparted on the potential brides."

"But she's so new to them. I doubt her lessons have included anything about the sacrament."

"That's probably the first lesson. The men coming here are warriors. We all want the same rite of marriage as our forefathers enjoyed. We need this."

"The humans don't understand the politics behind our coming here. They believe there is a fertility crisis, true, but not for the reason they believe. They don't understand the deeply intimate and entwining of what we expect. Some aren't coming for a dual marriage, but most are."

Jakkon nodded. "Your words are cold. Is your heart cold too? This cannot work if you are closing yourself off to her. Welcome your wife!" The pain and anger on his disfigured face stole Maxxen's breath.

I am dooming us. Jakkon was right. "Forgive me." He fought his embarrassed discomfort. "I -- this is not the way it should be."

"As always your anger lies at the heart of the issue." Jakkon's tone was heavy, but his chuckle made Maxxen's head jerk up. Their eyes met. "This is not easy for me either. This will not be easy for her. She is the one, but she doesn't understand just how important she is to our future. We need to make her feel her place with us. This goes beyond words. Resenting her for a wrong done by our society is not the way to begin."

Maxxen shook his head. "No. You're right," he muttered.

As always Jakkon's wisdom was astounding. Maxxen looked away. Jakkon stood up, and his long legs brought him quickly across the room. He put his hand on Maxxen's shoulder. They remained in a mute misery for a moment before Jakkon brightened.

"We should be celebrating. No harm has been done. She will be with us soon."

"Soon." So much weight lingered on that one word. Maxxen couldn't muster a smile. Darkness rose within his soul in the same place the memories of long gone battles lingered. "There is no reason to wait another moment. Have her brought on board. There is no turning back for the girl -- or us."

Jakkon nodded with one brisk motion before he left the room. Maxxen watched him go, and he remained in the dim room. Excitement rose within him, making him breathe faster and his heart ache with a fluttery tightness that reminded him of the moments before a battle. This was a war, after all, a fight for their ways, a challenge to the survival of true warriors. Mating this human girl -- woman -- was the only weapon they had against extinction.

It wasn't the soldiers who started the war, but they'd been the ones blamed when the dust had cleared. *Those bastard politicians -- they are the ones that deserve persecution.* But that wasn't the way of Xerra culture. He sighed, running his hand through his hair, and tried to force the darkness back. Slowly, his heart felt lighter as he imagined the girl from the video sitting on his veranda by the sea back home. She'd look lovely with the bright sun shining on her. *All I have to do is marry her.* Somehow that sounded more complicated than he thought it should.

Chapter Three

Shivering, Tegan stood alone in the darkness. "Hello?" The only sound was her heart thundering in her ears. "Hello?" Not only was it rude to leave a stranger in such an unwelcoming situation, but this conduct showed a level of disregard that made her regret signing her name on the contract. "At least wait for the ink to dry before you start pissing me off."

She'd been brought on board a space ship that was just as shiny and sterile as she'd expected. Their craft reminded her of every sci-fi movie she'd ever seen and instead of finding that comforting the thought was disconcerting. Usually, flesh eating space microbes or attacking tentacle-waving aliens appeared in those movies when everything seemed hunky dory. This is where the clueless human would die.

But now she'd been left alone in a dark, small room. Rage surfaced and evaporated her fear. She'd agreed to sign her name and leave her planet without the benefit of any ceremony. Now she was miles above the Earth, doomed to leave and never return, and she wanted out of the contract already. She'd been waiting for what felt like hours. Without a clock, she couldn't be sure just how long she'd been left in this cold place. Alone.

Shivering, Tegan began pacing. The room was large and empty. She looked for a weapon. The alien would consider her property. "What was I thinking?" She might not even be able to contact Beth when they arrived. Her sister could still be lost. "Why didn't I consider that before?"

A cold flash of fear washed over her, and her skin prickled. "Take me back! I changed my mind!" She paced faster. The wall slid open with a soft whoosh, and she turned to the shadowy figure entering. "I want to go back. I changed my mind." Panic welled inside of her, and she struggled to breathe. Her heart beat hard. All she knew was the man's name. Her husband, Maxxen, General of the First Order of the King's Trusted Protectors. His people didn't have last names. Job titles replaced names on Xerra.

According to the paperwork, she was now Tegan, Wife of the General and Best Swordsman. She assumed her new husband liked to brag. They could add a million titles and she'd never fit in. "Let me out of here!" Her panic returned as she thought of the new name. They'd taken everything from her. She closed her eyes and fought the sensation of the walls closing in on her in the darkness. Who could save her when she was trapped in the stars? "Please, I don't want this. I demand to be returned home!"

The tall form in the doorway didn't move. "You are mine. There is no going back."

Tegan's heart beat so fast pain radiated through her chest and arm. *Maybe I'm having a heart attack?* She took a few deep breaths trying to calm down. "You're Maxxen? Let me see you or take me back."

He chuckled. "Females don't make ultimatums on Xerra. It will take time for me to accept your idiosyncrasies."

"Idiosyncrasies! This isn't going to work. Return me to Earth. We've both made a terrible mistake." She took a step closer to him, trying to see him, but the darkness remained too thick. "Why are you hiding?" Her mouth went dry. *Am I married to a monster?*

"I watched many videos. Far too many to remember all the names and faces of the girls, but when I watched you, I knew you were the right choice." He stepped out of the shadows.

Tegan gasped. He was the most beautiful man she'd ever seen, but he wasn't tall like the other Xerraian males on the ship. The delivery boys who brought her onboard were gigantic. He was only a few inches taller than she was.

His face held an angelic beauty that made her think he should be a model-by-day rock-star-by night. His cheek bones were high, and his nose was straight and perfect in a way that somehow managed to be masculine. His wide set eyes were dark brown. The man's tan complexion complemented his wavy light brown hair. He had a pronounced Adam's apple and his shirt was open to expose his hair-less chest.

She could see he had a nice muscular abdomen and a sexy "V" pointing to places she hoped were as perfect as the rest of him. His very Xerraian baggy purple pants hung casually on his hips. This man's full, dark lips begged for kisses. Returning home was suddenly less appealing. Tegan licked her dry lips. *Oh. My. God. Is my mouth hanging open? Crap. Okay, I shut it, right? He's so hot he's melting my brain. Ugh.*

Tegan bit the inside of her cheek until it hurt just to be sure she wasn't hallucinating, sagged, and let out a breath she hadn't realized she'd been holding. "Why did you hide? You had me worried you had some terrible deformity you didn't disclose." *He's so hot. Why did he have to go all the way to Earth to find a woman? Any woman would want him.*

"You are not angry?" Maxxen pronounced in very careful English. One of his delicate dark brows rose. "Do you suffer a visual impairment?" He crossed his arms over his chest, waiting.

Tegan's nose wrinkled, and she shook her head. "With all the exams and paperwork, you have a very detailed record of my health history. My eyes are fine. What should I be mad about?"

"I am hardly of the correct -- stature -- to be a true warrior."

"You thought I'd expect you to be taller?" Tegan asked incredulously before tilting her head and watching the expressions play across his face. Confusion. Irritation. Anger. His reaction would be comical if she weren't so nervous. She swallowed, her throat suddenly dry, and then took a breath. "But you're so handsome I can't believe you thought height mattered. I didn't know what to expect, but I'm not disappointed." *Maybe being Mrs. Alien won't be so bad? Maybe?*

His eyes widened before they narrowed. "So you say." He crossed the room so that he stood right in front of her and seemed to be searching her expression. "I believed you would be honest. The devotion you show your sister made me respect you. Why lie to me?"

Tegan stomped her foot and glared. "How dare you? I am not lying, you insecure jerk. Take me home!"

Anger flared in his eyes, and he grabbed Tegan's biceps. She tilted her head to look up at him, and they glared for a long moment before he took a step back. He didn't hurt her, but she couldn't stop the tremor that ran through her as fear made her breath hitch.

Anger morphed into a neutrality as he gazed into her eyes. "You are mine. I -- We have started off wrong. My apologies. There are few I would trust. Only my brother-in-arms, Jakkon, has been my ally. Together we have picked our mate, you, we have traveled trillions of miles to make you ours."

Her stomach flip-flopped. *No. No. No. No.* She'd been duped. "I said one husband. I never signed up for a second."

"You are wrong. I have seen your signature. You agreed."

"I was lied to. I never knew I was signing up for that. Take me back."

The door opened again, and this time a goliath stepped into the room. Slowly, a dim yellow glow began radiating a soft light and created enough light to see clearly. Tegan took a step back. When the giant stepped into the light, he wasn't beautiful like Maxxen. His head was shaved. He wore a black leather vest and baggy red pants, tied snug at his waist. Tegan's breath caught in her throat as she took in his hulking form. His body was sculpted, but his bare skin bore a peppering of faint scars. The fierce face bore a scar from the temple to his chin. A chunk of his lip was missing as was part of his left ear. If it weren't for his kind green eyes, she'd have fainted as she gaped up at him.

"You consented and accepted your new name, Tegan, Wife of the General and Best Swordsman. Jakkon, your other husband, is our king's very best sword. I am his general," Maxxen replied. "Jakkon, our wife would like to change her mind."

"And what have you said to encourage her to stay?" Jakkon smiled, but it didn't reach his eyes. "I would not keep you by force. What future do you face on your return?" His English flowed a bit smoother than Maxxen's, but his lilting accent reminded her he wasn't a native speaker.

Tegan shrugged. "Not much of one. My government has ensured young, unmarried women are encouraged to be tested for marriage to your race if they don't have the education to get a good job or money to protect them. I have neither of those things and my sister left a few months ago. I learned that her new name is Beth, wife of Haggex."

"I do not know this Haggex, but I will do all I can to see that you have contact with her. We are not bad men." Jakkon stepped closer to her, dwarfing her so much she had to tilt her head all the way back to look up at him. "I would give you my heart if you would take it. I have lived many battles, and I hope to be done with that life. I seek harmony now."

Harmony sounded good. Tegan had spent so many years fighting to survive and to protect Beth she'd forgotten what peace was like. "I -- I don't want two husbands. One is going to be hard enough to get used to. You'd better take me back home."

"Take you back to a world you claim doesn't want you? I want you. Maxxen wants you. Think. Would you really go back and lose your sister? We will do what we can to make you happy."

Tegan bit her lip and glanced back and forth between the men. "Will you honestly help me find my sister?" Her resolve to return cracked.

They both nodded. "We respect truth, that was the reason we both agreed Maxxen had found the right woman in you," Jakkon said.

"What do you expect of me? These types of marriages are forbidden in my culture. I want to understand the dynamics before I agree to stay." Tegan was breathless as she finished.

Jakkon took her hand. For such a huge male, his touch was surprisingly gentle. "Follow us."

She looked around the room. Uncertainty made her feel as if she would suffocate as her panic welled up. "Can I go home?"

The men exchanged a look. Maxxen was the first to make eye contact with her. "No. We are already on our way to Xerra. You are ours."

She squeezed Jakkon's hand. When the big alien looked down at her the pity in his eyes made her throat tighten. "Tell me you won't hurt me. Tell me there's a chance for me to go home if I can't do this."

"You can handle this," he sounded certain. "Or we wouldn't have picked you. You are braver than you think. Come."

Conflicted, she followed them. She hadn't agreed to marry an alien because she thought she'd be madly in love, but she'd thought it would be different than this. She hoped she'd feel in control, but there was nothing about right now under her control. Jakkon's kind expression never wavered. Patience exuded from him to wash her in a wave of something akin to safety. Tegan nodded. Some of the tension left the big male.

Maxxen took her other hand. She glanced at their joined fingers. He gave her a grin, and she let the men lead her out of the room. If this was a horror movie, this was the scene where she'd suffer a gruesome death as the men turned into mutants.

"Do not look so afraid. We haven't eaten any brides this week," Jakkon said softly.

Tegan's back stiffened.

Maxxen cleared his throat. Jakkon scowled. "I jest with you. I have studied human culture and was taught amusement is often the way humans alleviate discomfort."

"Um, good try, but I was just thinking about how if this was a movie I'd probably die right about now."

Both men remained silent, which made the situation more awkward, as they continued to lead her down the well-lit corridor. Tegan's teeth chattered even though the temperature was perfect. She shivered. Nausea assailed her as a wave of hot then cold passed through her entire body. Fear affected her as a physical condition, and she took several deep breaths to gain control. *I can do this. I can do this. I can do this.* The mantra ran through her mind as the men ushered her into the unknown. These aliens -- her husbands -- couldn't have been more different. *What have I gotten myself into?* Given the opportunity, she'd run. Given the choice, she'd change her mind. Seeing the reality, she knew it was too late to go back. This was happening.

At the end of the hall were two huge doors. *Very unspaceship-like.* Something primal made the fear coil tighter inside of her, and she paused, unable to keep walking. Whatever waited behind those doors, she was pretty damn sure it wasn't a one-way ticket back to Earth.

Jakkon let go of her and opened the left door. The dark room slowly began to brighten. Maxxen let go of her arm to open the right side. Tegan peered through the dimness to see a lavish spectacle. The room was sunken, and steps led to what looked like a strange mattress on the floor. The area was piled with pillows and throw blankets. It appeared -- inviting -- and somehow unspeakably terrifying at the same time. Tegan did her best not to turn around and run away from the men and the elegant depravity entry into that portal offered. Her mouth went dry.

"Come," Maxxen ordered, holding his hand out to her. She looked at the extended limb and back at the man's face. The way his mouth compressed told her this was a man that was used to being obeyed. She'd never been one to comply with an order. Her back stiffened and her chin tilted up a notch.

Jakkon glanced between Tegan and Maxxen. He sighed. "Please. Come into the temple."

"Temple?" Tegan tried to swallow around the lump in her throat. *Like the room wasn't scary enough before.* "I don't want to go in there."

"I can see that," Jakkon spoke with measured patience. "I assure you nothing will happen to you that will cause you harm or distress. If you become -- unhappy -- at any time just tell us so."

"So, my safe word is unhappy?"

"Safe word?" Maxxen's eyes narrowed. "I did not realize how superstitious your people are. You believe the word holds power?"

Tegan rolled her eyes. "No, but I, um, I need to be sure you understand if I want you to stop."

Jakkon put his hand on her shoulder, very lightly, and when she looked up at him, his face his lips turned up and his eyes crinkled at the corners. There was something warm in his expression. "If you say stop, we will respect your request. There are many years ahead of us, and I would not wish to start out with fear or pain."

As Tegan looked up into his gentle eyes, she realized she liked Jakkon. Maxxen was beautiful on the outside, but he lacked something empathetic that the disfigured giant had in abundance.

Jakkon put his arm around her and pulled her close to him. The fact she didn't feel the urge to pull away registered briefly, but she noticed the sandalwood scent of him and calmed a bit. Strangely, the huge man made her feel safe. Her racing heart slowed. "I will let no harm come to you, my wife. You have my word."

My wife. She still couldn't think of herself in that way. The name of wife was surreal, and she couldn't wrap her brain around the change in her status. "Why are we going into your temple?"

He gazed into her eyes with an intensity strong enough to heat to her cheeks. "I would honor you by giving you a proper marriage. Something more than your signature, but not quite the full..." He seemed to be struggling for a word. "*Ra Mah Gjia.*"

Tegan blinked up at him blankly. "*Ra Mah Gjia?*"

"Pomp and circumstance," Maxxen supplied. "This is a modified ceremony, mostly for Jakkon's benefit. He felt we would dishonor you without it."

Tegan reached out and put her hand over Jakkon's, where it rested on her shoulder, before looking up at him. "Thank you. I don't need something. I was never the little girl who dreamed of a fairy tale wedding."

"Fairy tale?" Jakkon asked.

"Special... magical. That's not something I need to fulfill my commitment. I just want to be safe and not feel so out of my control. Being forced into everything is what scares me."

Maxxen let go of the door he still held open. He looked a little self-conscious, glancing away from her and frowning, but then he stepped forward and took her hand. He met her gaze. "I understand that need. I too suffer from the desire to control my future. I am not a tender man, but I will do my best."

His declaration was almost sweet. Tegan squeezed his fingers. "Thank you. I -- I will stay." *I have nothing and no one to go back to.* They seem to care. She shrugged. "I will do my best."

A smile lit up Maxxen's face making him even handsomer. "Wonderful!"

Jakkon still had his arm around her. "Come," he whispered leaning down close to her head. "Let us be one."

One. The concept filled her with something akin

to excitement, yet flavored with trepidation. One. Three in a marriage seemed like a crowd. "Okay." She spoke so softly the words barely had any strength.

* * *

"Are you sure about this?" Maxxen asked. He didn't want her to have any regrets. He sure as hell wouldn't. He and Jakkon exchanged a look that said they needed her to be willing.

Jakkon led her inside. Her gaze darted all around, and he tried to imagine what the room looked like to her human eyes. The ceiling was high. Tiny lights twined with long multi-hued flowing scarves. Each strip drifted down from the center of the room in artful billows of color and light. The door opened, and they stepped onto the square platform that followed the circumference of the space. Four levels moved down the room, following the square, to create stairs. In the center of the sunken space a large El Lamire -- ceremonial bed filled the space. Pillows and colorful throws decorated the sacred space. Symbols as ancient as his people sprinkled the walls telling of ancient love stories and promises of family and peace.

With two men protecting their woman and children they could breathe easy when leaving home, knowing the other was there. Two strong hearts beating in time with the one they loved -- this was the path of happiness for a warrior. Finding a woman who was biologically compatible this far from home was worth the long trip. Finding a woman whose heart was compatible was priceless. Tegan was everything he'd ever wanted. She was the completion of Soul Trinity. Her every breath was a gift, and her existence was the embodiment of the dream he'd had since coming of age. One day, hopefully soon, she'd become his sanctuary.

Berggan, a trusted brother in arms, sat waiting quietly in the room. They'd brought him for the purpose of witnessing and because he was curious about what kind of women Earth had to offer. Tegan gasped when she saw the man. He'd done his queries at the agency where they'd found Tegan. But ever the pessimist, Breggan was undecided if this was the path he wanted to follow.

"Berggan is here as witness to the vow, nothing else," Maxxen assured his bride.

Jakkon chuckled. "Truly, four is a crowd on a wedding night."

The scarlet flush that colored Tegan's cheeks charmed him. Maxxen longed to kiss her heated face until the flush rose from desire instead of discomfort. He wanted to love her until nothing mattered but their mating.

Jakkon led her down the stairs, she still gazed wide-eyed at Berggan, but allowed herself to be led to the sunken area of the room. She stood awkwardly between himself and Jakkon. He wanted to make this right for her, but on instinct, he needed to claim her fully. He'd spent too many years dreaming of her. The time for action was upon them.

"Today my soul will unite with yours." Maxxen took her hand. "Jakkon's soul will unite with yours. You will feel our needs, our fears and you will be the cornerstone of the life we build. Do you have the courage to become part of our soul trinity?"

"What choice do I have?" Tegan asked.

Jakkon grimaced before clearing his throat. "None, but I will not take you by force or against your will. If you deny this union, we will send you home."

"We will not!" Maxxen countered. Anger flared in him. She was the one. He would not be denied.

"We will." Jakkon insisted.

Maxxen's anger died as he saw the fear in her eyes. A protective instinct roared to life inside of him. He'd keep her from sadness even if it meant a piece of his soul had to die. He realized he was ready to give her everything, even his happiness.

* * *

Tegan glanced between the men. They were her only real option. "Yes." The men turned to gawk at her. "I accept you. Both of you."

"Tegan Blake has agreed to the union of souls. Tonight, on this ship, we bind her to our hearts with our bodies. If any would stop this occurrence, they must act before the bell tolls."

There was no one there but the creepy guy in the back. No one was going to step in to save her from this decision. A bell chimed. *Oh my God, it's done.*

She hadn't noticed the cup and wine bottle on the step until Maxxen picked up the silver chalice.

He held the cup up. "I claim Tegan Blake." Then he took a long drink before handing the cup to Jakkon.

"I too claim Tegan Blake." Jakkon took an equally long drink.

Jakkon held the cup out to her, and she gingerly accepted the cold metal. The liquid inside was green and smelled almost floral. She scowled into the mystery booze before glancing up at her alien husbands.

"Drink," Maxxen urged.

Tegan obeyed. The vile potion was sour, and she sputtered, but managed a single swallow.

"Tegan, Wife of the General and Best Swordsman, we welcome you to our lives and promise you our protection and love," Jakkon said.

Maxxen took the cup from her hands. "We give

you security and promise to cherish you today and every day we draw breath."

The stranger who'd waited in the room stood, walked down the stairs, and kissed her gently on each cheek. He kissed her forehead too. The large man had warm brown eyes. "It has been witnessed." He clasped the forearms of each of her new husbands and then went up the stairs and out of the temple without a backward glance.

She waited. Nothing happened. Gooseflesh rose on her arms. "What now?" she whispered.

Jakkon swept her into his arms, and she yelped with surprise. He gazed down into her face. "Now. We make love to our wife until she is fully satisfied and knows our bodies and we know hers. Today is the first day of a lifetime of passion, sweet wife." He pressed his lips to hers in a chaste, brief contact.

Tegan gazed up at him, uncertain, and yet sure what she did next would affect the rest of her life. She took his face between her hands and kissed him with feeling. Her eyes fluttered closed, and she put all her fear and desperation into that contact. She conveyed just how lonely she was with every second of the kiss. Jakkon held her tighter, groaning. His powerful body put her down on the large floor mattress with care that managed both sweet and reassuring.

"I -- I don't know what the IBP might have promised you, but I'm not a virgin. I've never had sex with two men. Help me not do it wrong."

Maxxen knelt beside her. "There is no wrong in this. There is no shame of past encounters. The bell is symbolic of renewal. The past died away when it rang. There is you, and there is us. After what we do here all that will be left is we. We are married, and we will love, Tegan. You are a new person. You are... ours."

He seemed to struggle at the end, but his elegant explanation promised this would be powerful instead of degrading. Relief flooded her.

She nodded mutely. Maxxen didn't ask for permission as he leaned over her and unbuttoned her blouse. He pushed the fabric off her shoulders. Her bra was the serviceable white one they'd supplied her with when she'd been given her IBP uniform.

Chapter Four

The Earth garment wasn't meant to be sexy, but Maxxen thought this was right for his new wife. She was the kind of woman who would be practical in all things, even her undergarments. Yet, there was a wildness inside of her he desired to unlock. He slipped one of the straps off her shoulder and deposited a tender kiss. She lay stiff when he kissed her neck. Jakkon rubbed the sacred pressure point on the back of her wrist, and she seemed to relax as Maxxen gazed down at her. "We'll take this slow," he said.

"Okay," she whispered.

Maxxen pushed the front clasp of her bra together, and it opened to expose her beautiful, small breasts, He cupped them, and his cock strained against his pants. She gasped and arched into his hold. He rubbed his thumbs over her nipples and listened to the music of her whimpers.

"Touching you is a pleasure, wife. Would you like more of my touch?"

She nodded, pressing her lips together and closing her eyes. Maxxen released her long enough to untie the string at his waist. The material pooled around his knees. She still had her eyes closed. He squeezed her nipples firmly, and she arched her back, whimpering. He pressed her back against the mattress, gently.

Jakkon stood watching. The man untied his drawstring and the fabric whispered to the floor with a flutter. The big man stepped away from the clothing, and Maxxen stifled the twinge of jealousy the larger man's erection gave him. Loving his wife, in his own way, would have to make up for his modest size.

According to his research, his cock was

impressive by Earth's standards, but that didn't make him feel any better about the fact that he didn't measure up to Jakkon. *Will she love him more?* Jealousy in Soul Trinity was the greatest failure, and he fought the ugly emotion away. *I will not fail her. I will not let this destroy what we can have.* Taking a calming breath, he put his focus where it belonged, on Tegan.

She wore a very Earth-style skirt that matched the blouse. He pushed the material up, so it gathered at her hips and left her long pale legs bare. The simple white cotton panties matched the bra. He liked that, a lot. Maxxen pulled them down next. Her pussy was natural. The smell of her desire encouraged him. She wasn't too afraid of them to respond to what he was doing. He liked that too. Her eyes flew open, and she was watching him regard her.

"You're beautiful," he said and tenderly parted her thighs to kneel between her legs. She allowed him to open her wide.

"I -- I haven't done this in a while," she stammered. "Is it different on your world? I -- I'm not sure if I'm... If I'm ready yet."

Maxxen chuckled. "I'm not going to unite us so callously. Do the men of Earth not enjoy their women? Has no man ever prepared you mind, body, and soul for his penetration?" He could already see she was glistening, wet for him. He could understand how men might be so overcome with need that they took their own pleasure, but he had a warrior's resolve. "I have vowed to cherish you. My body will enjoy yours, but my soul will only be complete if you enjoy mine as well. I would never take from you without giving you something in return."

His beautiful young wife flushed. "Thank you for being considerate."

"Oh, sweet wife, I shall thank you by worshiping your body. Sex is a sacred act. Only a man without honor wouldn't understand the power and beauty of a woman's orgasm."

She bit her lip. Embarrassment and shame played across her face, but he saw that her body still glistened and a flush spread over her pale breasts. Biology worked even as her human thoughts kept her fixated on her planet's strange views about sex.

This must be odd for a woman to give herself to two warriors who gain strength and higher awareness from orgasm when her culture has so many rules against pleasure. "There is nothing -- bad -- about what we are about to do. You are giving Jakkon and me the greatest gift any woman can. You give us strength."

Tegan's flush darkened, but she nodded, and his gaze never left hers as he spread her thighs. Maxxen glanced at his friend and grinned. Jakkon nodded and found his place between her legs. He lapped at their woman's pussy. She bucked her hips and arched her back as he pleasured her. Maxxen went to her breasts and loved them with tenderness. Tegan's little mewling protests became whimpers of pleasure. Her cries grew. She thrashed.

Jakkon lapped faster, harder. He gazed up at her. Her blue eyes remained shut tight, but she ground her needy body against Jakkon's mouth and tangled her fingers in his hair, bucking against his face. Tegan cried out, and Maxxen sucked a nipple into his mouth, hard. Her back arched. *I can feel her heart beating. I know she feels the Soul Trinity.*

"Jakkon!" A long, unintelligible sound followed her cry. "Maxxen!"

Maxxen took her in his arms, kissing her face and smoothing hair away from her eyes and mouth. He murmured his affection and encouragement in their mother tongue.

Jakkon didn't let her rest after she came, and continued tormenting her with his mouth. She writhed under him, bucking and thrashing. All the while, she mewed a desperate plea for relief. He gave her none. Leaving her wanting wouldn't make her theirs. She'd give them both everything if she wanted them.

Jakkon sucked loudly on her clit. Maxxen watched, and his cock ached for attention. She gasped. Tears wet her cheeks with the intensity of what he made her feel. Maxxen kissed away each trace of her pleasurable suffering, and when he put his mouth on hers, she wrapped her arms around his neck and kissed him back with a passion she hadn't shown yet.

Maxxen never broke the kiss, but his hand slid down her stomach and down her hip. He snaked his hand between her body and Jakkon's head until he found her wet pussy. Maxxen slipped a finger inside her hungry cunt, and her muscles reacted. He slipped a second inside her, and she moaned into his mouth. He wiggled his fingers so that he rubbed against the bumpy spot women always seemed to respond to and his wife was no exception. She jerked and gasped against his lips. He moved faster, twisting his fingers just a bit. Her breathing came faster. She held him to her mouth like he was the air she needed to live. That was the moment Maxxen released her, finger fucking her faster and making her come because she was theirs. He pulled his mouth away, and she threw her head back, grunting a shout of ecstasy. Maxxen watched her orgasm, and he heard Jakkon lapping her pussy with greedy abandon. Something akin to hope blossomed in his heart. They would be okay. This would be okay.

Tegan's pleasure ebbed. Jakkon stopped his oral

activities, and as if sensing his eyes on her she fluttered her long lashes and opened her eyes, looking from Jakkon to Maxxen and back again. He grinned. Jakkon moved to take her in his arms. Maxxen let her go, a little reluctantly, as Jakkon began kissing her behind the ear.

Without a word, Tegan bent to Maxxen's waist, taking his cock in her mouth, and sucked him, hard. She shielded him from her teeth. He groaned. She awed him. He closed his eyes and exhaled.

"Wonderful," he encouraged in English before muttering an endearment in his own language. He resisted taking a fist full of her hair in his hand. *Gentle, she's human.* He closed his eyes and moaned. *That's incredible.* Tegan. His wife, giving him just what he needed, this was what Soul Trinity was meant to be. His heart swelled as his balls tightened. "I am too close," he growled. "Your mouth -- beautiful torment."

Tegan released him. The tip of her tongue slid over her bottom lip, and he had the strong urge to suck on that lip.

Maxxen pulled her up and took her in his arms. Jakkon rubbed her back. Maxxen looked into her eyes and just gazed at how beautiful his young human wife was. He pressed his mouth to hers, kissing his woman breathless and sucking on her lower lip.

Maxxen positioned her so he could kneel between her legs. She was on her hands and knees compliant and trusting. He ran his hand over her soft pale ass cheek before he dropped a kiss where his hand had been. He knelt behind her and the scent of her desire perfumed the air. "I'm going to make love to you unless you've changed your mind." He'd honor her decision.

"I want you inside me," she said in a breathy

voice that sent a shock of desire right to his cock.

* * *

She couldn't believe she was begging him for this. She would have done anything for them in that moment. They owned her in a way she'd never let another man own her, and she didn't care. She wanted -- needed more.

Maxxen moved so that he could pump a large, long finger inside of her as his tongue lavished attention on her clit. His face was buried between her thighs, and his tongue delved into her pussy. Need raged hotter inside of her womb. Maxxen continued to work on her pussy, and she cried out into Jakkon's mouth as he pulled her to him for a kiss. She came then, ferociously. Her screams were devoured by the giant's kiss as he fondled her breasts. Jakkon cupped them tenderly and flicked her nipples with his thumbs.

Tegan moaned. She felt his mouth on her left breast. His lips were cold; she shivered as he drew hard on the sensitive peak. Maxxen still lavished with attention between her legs. Pleasure burned lower, and she mewed little whimpers as the fire burned to embers and then blazed hot again. Maxxen pulled her hips back, and Tegan gasped as she felt his cock rest on her ass cheek. Her pussy convulsed. She'd come, but she wanted more. The men's lust flowed through her giving her no relief even after her satisfaction had been reached, leaving her to suffer in an endless cycle of reprieve and desire. His thumb rubbed her clit while his index finger delved inside to caress her g-spot.

Her vision was a haze of lust. He pulled his hand away, and she groaned with disappointment. Heat came from deep inside of her. Prickles of awareness stirred in her as her pussy tingled, reminding her she wanted him to fill the emptiness there. The man grabbed her around her waist and pulled her back toward his erection. Her pussy convulsed in anticipation. His erection was proof of his desire as the large cock slid over skin, so close to her pussy, but not nearly close enough.

"I can feel your heart beating with my heart," Maxxen said. "You awe me, human." His voice warmed her. "Give me your soul, woman, give us your heart," he whispered.

Maxxen's lips descended into a punishing kiss. He left her breathless and wanting. She'd been kissed by human men, but never like this. No other man or men inspired such desperation as these two men, her husbands, stirred in her.

Tegan bit her lip as Maxxen put his mouth on her nipple and sucked hard. His hand was between her legs, strumming her pleasure points. She nodded and took a deep breath, whimpering.

"Tell us you're ours." Maxxen moved so quickly she had no time to think as he rolled her to her back and pinned her hands above her head. She lay trapped on the mattress, and her heart thundered in her ears. Jakkon was there beside her, he caressed her face, raining kisses on her, before running his hands softly down her torso. Her new husbands stared at her as if she was the most amazing thing they'd ever seen. She could feel a blush rising up her neck.

Maxxen continued to hold her in place. Tegan managed a half-hearted struggle, until he spread her legs with his knee. Wild lust rekindled her desire, and she spread as wide as she could. "You make me so wet," she said in a hoarse voice. "Mmm, so wet. Touch me again. I'm dying… I'll die without -- more." Being helpless under him was erotic. If he wasn't holding her arms, she'd touch herself. "I need to be fucked! Ooh, please." She flushed as tears formed in her eyes. She couldn't breathe.

Maxxen held her tighter as Jakkon moved between her legs and snuggled his head between her spread thighs. She felt him lick her inner thigh. She gazed into Maxxen's face, and he grinned down wickedly. The strangeness melted away as her entire being told her she belonged to both of them. Her body came alive with sensation. When Jakkon's hands reached up to play with her sensitive nipples the combination of pleasures was amazing. A moan escaped her lips. Maxxen pressed a kiss to her mouth, and she opened for his tongue to explore. He smothered her moans with his fervent kiss.

Maxxen continued the passionate assault and yearning built until the want erupted in flames. Maxxen let go of her arms, and his touch roamed over her breasts. Jakkon's mouth worked tirelessly between her spread legs until she thrashed. Her sobs came unhindered. Nothing could be better than this!

"We can give you what you need, but first we have to know we possess you, Tegan. Are you ours?" Maxxen's voice echoed in her ears.

Jakkon looked up at her. "Tell us," he demanded as he continued flicking her clit and nipping the tender nub. Every sensation pushed her ever closer to the edge. She bucked wildly with no concern for propriety.

"Please, Jakkon," she begged.

Jakkon held his erection, guiding his length so that he nudged her opening. Tegan pressed against him without encouragement, so he rubbed her slick clit with his hard cock. She arched her back, and a soft gasp danced over his ears. He rubbed her harder and faster. Her hands clutched the sheet. She tried to impale herself on him, but he moved.

"Please," she begged.

Jakkon paused, and her frustration mounted. "Tell us," he insisted.

Tegan pushed up towards Jakkon with her hips. She rubbed her wet pussy against his stubbled chin crying out in frustration and pleasure as the sensitive area brushed his rough face. She gasped, wanting more.

"Say the words," Maxxen ordered, pinching her nipples, hard. Arching her back, she shamelessly ground against Jakkon's face.

"I give in."

"That's not what I want. Say the words," Maxxen coaxed. He kissed her neck. Then Jakkon kissed her pussy causing her to groan with pleasure.

"I'm yours." She panted. Maxxen's longer fingers delved into her pussy while his thumb rolled against her clitoris. "I'm so close," Tegan replied breathlessly. Maxxen gave her nipple a quick pinch, but then Jakkon returned to suck her clit between his teeth, and she cried out as he began lapping at her furiously. Tegan pressed her thighs gently against his head. Her body wanted him to do what he was doing harder. She arched up, grinding her pussy against his mouth.

"I -- I need more," she pleaded. "Fuck me!"

"Don't fight it. Relax," Maxxen said.

Moaning, and on the verge of orgasm, she followed his orders.

Jakkon pulled away the moment she started to come and panic swelled in her. She needed this so much. Maxxen moved so that he hovered over her; his cock was between her legs and in a swift thrust Tegan was filled with him. "You were made for me," he told her quietly, and then he arched his back gasping. He thrust fast, hard, and she screamed as her delayed gratification poured through her like a tsunami of joy. She felt the heat of his release spurt inside of her.

Maxxen's fingers moved faster, and Tegan cried out. Maxxen whispered her name as he collapsed next to her.

Maxxen didn't give her time to recover before he moved to straddle her again with his glorious, muscular body. He loomed as his cock drove deeply into her body. Her pussy contracted instantly and knew it wouldn't take much to come again her sensitivity peaking. She gripped him with her inner muscles and bucked wildly against him, screaming his name as their bodies collided in a sweaty dance. His face looked strained, but he had amazing stamina.

Stroke after stroke he didn't come, and she kept crying out, shaking and gasping from the intensity -- pleasure so great it was becoming painful. Never before had she felt such bliss, that she found herself weeping. Jakkon was there instantly, holding her, tenderly pushing the hair off her face. Tegan lay panting. The smell of sex perfumed the air. Jakkon took his mouth off her nipple, she rolled her head to the side, to look at him. He leaned over and placed a kiss on her mouth. Maxxen didn't let her pull away as he grabbed her hips and tugged her closer. He studied her flushed, sleepy face. She looked spent.

Maxxen entered her with cautious precision. Jakkon fondled her dangling breasts as Maxxen pushed into her until he filled her. He began slowly, but her whimpered pleas quickened his pace. Jakkon kept one hand on her breast, and the other found her clit. He worked with Maxxen to give her maximum pleasure, and when she came, Maxxen relished the sound. Experiencing the resonation of her orgasm through their mating was spiritual on a level no other sex matched. His whole body shook as he held back his release. Maxxen roared as he lost the battle and came.

Tegan's pussy convulsed around him, milking every drop of his pleasure. When it was over, he rested his forehead against her back and let out a sated sigh.

"You're incredible." Maxxen kissed the small of her back. His heart and soul had never made love with a woman until Tegan. Every other woman had just been sex. This was beyond the scope of his experience.

"It is my turn, brother, my time to be strengthened by her body and soul," Jakkon said. Maxxen ran his hand down her back before moving away. Tegan remained kneeling, panting. "We will couple in the ancient way."

Jakkon took Tegan in his arms and she, limp with release, she was putty in his hands. He laid back and moved her, so she straddled his massive erection. Her eyes widened, and she stiffened when she noticed his size.

"All will be well," Jakkon whispered to her. "You control this. You set the pace." The pads of his fingers brushed her nipples as he took her breasts in his hands. He stroked them until she groaned and arched into his touch. Then his fingers moved to skim her sides before his palms rubbed against her back. He pulled her close, and his erection pressed against her belly as his cock jutted up between them.

Chapter Five

Tegan forced her expression to show no fear as she reached out and took his length in her hand. He was hard, and the velvet sensation of his skin in her palm was silken steel. He was disfigured, but his dick was beautiful. Too big, way too scary big, but beautiful nonetheless. She stroked him in a slow rhythm, and he growled deep in his throat. The massive male grinned, and she realized she did have control after all. Sex was dominance. Giving him pleasure was power. She owned her newfound supremacy as she watched his eyes half close and darken with lust.

Jakkon pulled her down, fast, to meet his mouth as he groaned with pleasure. One of his large hands cupped the back of her head while his mouth savaged hers with animalistic passion. His fingers tangled in her loose hair as he clutched her to him.

Tegan trailed her right hand down his shoulder and chest and traced the defined muscles of his abdomen. She tracked his scars. *So many scars.* He pulled her up so his mouth could reach her breast, and he kissed her nipple reverently before drawing it in and sucking hard.

She gasped and moaned until he released her and repeated the process on the other breast. Her breath came out in little gasps when he found her clit, and she hovered over him. Jakkon pleasured her with skill and tenderness. She didn't know what she'd expected, but this wonderful waltz of sensations wasn't it.

He helped her to kneel over him again, and her fingers found the length of his cock, she tightened her grip with careful precision. He sucked in a breath and let it out with a groan that was almost a sigh. She explored his erection and sac with her fingers. Pleasure made her shiver as Maxxen joined in and ran his teeth over her left nipple. She closed her eyes and rubbed her hand faster up and down Jakkon's length.

Maxxen moved to devour her other nipple, drawing it into his mouth.

She cupped Jakkon's sac, and his quick inhaled breath told her he liked what she was doing.

"I want you inside me." Her voice was strained with raw need as she looked down into Jakkon's eyes.

"Are you sure you're ready? I've waited a long time, and I can wait longer. I know I am... larger than a human male. I want you to have only memories of pleasure with me, especially this first sacred time. When I mate you, I want you to experience bliss."

Tegan nodded fiercely and bit her lip. "I'll be careful. Like you said, I'm in control."

Jakkon groaned and nodded. He was so gentle when he reached up and cupped her cheek. She didn't know what to do with the emotions bubbling up inside her. Tears prickled behind her eyelids.

She rose, straddling him and hovering just over his massive erection. Her body was slick with her desire and Maxxen's release. Jakkon held the base of his big cock, and she gingerly pressed her opening against him, taking the head of his cock inside her. Inch by thick inch she slid down him, gasping and moaning at the fullness. She stopped above where he held himself. She looked down into his eyes. "I -- I can't take it all."

"You are so tight," he moaned. "I have no complaint. You are a gift from the gods."

She moved on him, slowly. His eyes closed and his expression was strangely strained while retaining a peaceful repose. Maxxen helped her balance while at the same time playing with her breasts. The sensation heightened her pleasure. She moved faster, wilder. Jakkon groaned but didn't come. She moved faster up and down his shaft. Maxxen squeezed her nipples and pain/pleasure mingled with the sensation of Jakkon's cock rubbing inside of her in just the right way. The rhythmic motion forced a long moan from her.

"Jakkon," she wailed. "I'm so close." She hovered on the brink of another orgasm. *I'm his -- theirs!*

Jakkon groaned as she rode him. His left hand stayed at her breast, but his right hand snaked down to find her clit. He rubbed her pleasure point as her tight heat slid up and down on his length. Jakkon's hips matched the rhythm she set. He thrust deeply inside her as she rode him.

When she came this time, she sobbed his name like a prayer. Jakkon's eyes closed and he threw back his head. The heat of his orgasm filled her. But they weren't done with her yet. Jakkon rolled her onto her hands and knees and caressed her back and shoulders as Maxxen thrust inside of her. To her delight, the pleasure rekindled. He held her hips and took her hard. Every thrust hit her at the perfect angle. His body fit hers perfectly, and his stamina brought unshed tears that blurred her vision.

Tegan hadn't thought it possible, but she was ready to come again. "I'm so close," she wailed.

Maxxen pumped into her. Tegan had no complaints as the pleasure built until another orgasm pulled a cry out of her. He wrapped her hair around his hand and pulled her head back. She was pliable and submissive as he kissed her neck, and she wailed with the force of her release. Jakkon's hands ran over her, and he whispered soft sounds of comfort. He supported her when her arms started shaking. Tegan reveled in her gratification, nothing mattered but sensation as she rode out this final, explosive orgasm.

Behind her closed eyelids, she saw sparks. Her pussy clenched and she wailed as the indescribable power of the carnal thrill assaulted her senses, and her orgasm stretched out until Maxxen collapsed. Jakkon helped her to lay down on her stomach on the huge mattress. She breathed in the men's scents and something floral from the sheets. Jakkon lay on her left and Maxxen on her right. She wrapped her arms around Jakkon's neck and kissed him softly as Maxxen kissed her neck and shoulders.

Peace.

For the first time in her life there was no anxiety, only a sense of safety and relaxation.

When Jakkon pulled back to look at her, she blinked up at him sleepily. She yawned widely. "What happens now?" she mumbled as she lay her head on his chest.

He ran his hand through her hair. "Now we go home. Have some offspring, and live as we choose. I swear to you we'll care for you all the days of your life."

She hadn't meant quite that far ahead. "I mean, where do we sleep?"

Maxxen kissed her back. "Together. Some couples keep separate rooms, but I would like the three of us to be united in all things."

"I agree." Tegan felt the words rumble from him under her cheek. "Do we sleep here?"

Maxxen laughed at her question. "The temple is good for many things, but sleeping isn't one of them. We will return here for love making after we've feasted and rested. It would be very good luck to conceive in the temple." He dropped a kiss on her flat stomach. "And the sooner, the better. I'm not getting any younger."

Panic welled up. "This feels too fast. Are you sure I'm even able to have your children?"

"We're very sure. You're going to be a wonderful mother. Our people have -- talents -- not known to those on Earth. When we made love, I saw our path. You're a wonderful mother -- or will be," Jakkon said.

Tegan's mouth went dry. "You... saw? Kids?"

"Yes. We're going to be very happy. Don't worry so much, wife."

"That's easy for you to say Mr. Crystal Ball."

"Mr. Crystal Ball? Who is this Crystal Ball?" Jakkon's tone held a note of jealousy.

Tegan chuckled. "A crystal ball is a device used to see the future -- it's fake. It's an Earth phrase. Can everyone on your planet see the future?" Her drowsiness evaporated as wonder left her invigorated.

"No. Soul Trinity brings about changes in us. You've given me strength. I have never felt so strong. I'm so filled with you that I could fight an army, alone, and win. There are many benefits for all of us. In time, you will see our marriage for the magic and blessing it is. Our bond is far more than a legal contract." Maxxen turned her to look at him. "You mean more to us than just a signature on paper."

"I believe you," she said she kept her voice even and gave him one firm nod. "Why did you have to come all the way to Earth? I heard talk of issues with reproduction, but whenever the subject was broached the IBP always breezed over the topic. I've never gotten a satisfying answer."

"Soul Trinity threatens the government," Jakkon whispered in her ear. "Because it makes warriors stronger and a true warrior is conceived in a trinity. Our way of life is being eradicated."

"But they allow you to come to Earth and bring wives back?"

"They do, but the time and expense make this a desperate measure. Few women capable of mating in a trinity will. It's become socially unacceptable to be married to a warrior and even more so to be in Soul Trinity with two." Maxxen brushed the hair out of her eyes. "We came a long way to find you and make our hearts whole."

"Great," Tegan mumbled. "I get to go from one world that doesn't want me to another that won't."

"We want you. We'll give you everything we have. You and our children will be protected." Jakkon kissed her temple. "We live in the last city that believes in the old ways and will accept us. You'll have the chance to see human immigrants."

Hope that she'd see her sister again flared in her heart. Trepidation encroached on her excitement when she realized one city was not all of their world. "Do you think I'll see Beth? I have another friend who's been married. Her name is Alexa."

"I can't promise you'll see your sister, but I know Alexa's husbands. They are good men, leaders, and strong warriors. You'll see your friend. There is a battle coming, a fight for our love. Will you give us your strength?"

"Yes." Tegan was amazed at how easily the response came for her. She was part of them now. There was no undoing what'd been done. "You have it now and as long as you want it."

Maxxen kissed her soft and quick. "We would die for you, but it will not come to that. When we get home to Xerra we will fight for what we've found."

She snuggled into Maxxen's arms. Jakkon's warm body infused her back with heat, and his arms came around to hold her. "I'm yours." She closed her eyes. There might be trouble ahead, but for now, she was happy just to let these men love her. Tegan sighed.

They held her tighter, and she knew they loved her. "I lied." Heat warmed her cheeks. "I can love you -- both of you."

Maxxen took her face between his hands, with infinite tenderness, and gazed into her eyes. "I -- we love you. I am astonished at how quickly you have become the breath in my lungs and the whole of my soul. Thank you for being our wife."

She blinked away the tears that had come unbidden to her eyes. Her throat clogged.

Jakkon cleared his throat. "You have given us everything we could ever want." His deep voice rumbled against her shoulder. "And we're ready to give you the universe."

Tegan relaxed into the warm cocoon of her husbands as the reminder they were speeding through space entered her brain. She grinned. Even if the path promised a bumpy journey, she was ready for adventure.

Shaalon (Married To The Aliens 3)
Ashlynn Monroe

Shaalon knows she made a mistake defying her king, but she never thought she'd be sacrificed to an alien. Thrust in a cell with a bloodthirsty male of Xerra's warrior class, she expects a terrible death. Bracing for the worst, she never expects to find hope in his eyes.

Cayylen wanted a warrior's death, not the disgrace of an execution. With a single sun cycle left to him, his last request is to be given the daughter of his enemy. He never expects his request to be honored, but the moment he looks in Shaalon's eyes he realizes she is his mate.

The strength Cayylen gains from finding his woman is enough for him to break free, but he refuses to let her go. War has been coming for a long time, but will taking his woman hostage be the tipping point the warriors need to fight the system trying to end their lines?

Chapter One

Shaalon struggled against the rough hands dragging her down the long corridor. *How did I let this happen?* Her mind whirled with the events that had led to this moment. *Her execution.* She closed her eyes and went limp under her captors' hold. The scent of mildew and the sound of water dripping softly provided a dark ambiance for her execution.

One of the men shook her. "Get moving!" Tears prickled behind her eyelids as she tried to delay this journey as long as possible. The sudden blow to her cheek took her by surprise. Her eyes flew open, and she tasted blood. She glared at the grinning male to her left.

"You shouldn't have defied your king." His tone showed no sympathy or remorse.

"For defending a pregnant woman, who only wanted her family safe, I should die?" she asked, incredulously. "Her husband was a prisoner because he believed in different gods than the king does. We must stop this genocide."

The other man yanked her so hard she lost her footing. The painful hold on her biceps was the only reason she didn't tumble head first into the rock wall.

"She was a traitor, as is anyone who supports that kind of thinking. She believed in the Mother spirit. Did no one tell you that? Warriors once served a purpose, but those times are over," said the man who had slapped her. "The kingdom needs our new religion, not the antiquated way of warriors and polyamory."

She didn't say how his kind of singular thinking was dangerous. Nothing good ever came of all or nothing mentalities. Her father fought for the king. He was no warrior, but he was proud to be a good soldier. He couldn't have known how the king's tyranny would change their world. Father still believed in free will.

She lost her footing, and the men let her go. With her hands shackled behind her back, she was helpless to break her fall. They laughed. She cried out as pain radiated through her right arm and torso. The hateful mirth echoed in her head and she had to clamp her mouth shut to avoid saying something that would make her captors more violent.

The shorter man hauled her to her feet, pointing to a broad set of doors. "Smell that? That's the blood of traitors. That's where we should be taking you." Shaalon's stomach turned at the smell as they walked past the execution room. She refused to look, even when the men paused at the door. A scream rent the silence, making her cringe.

One of the men chuckled darkly. "You could learn something here. Like when to keep your mouth shut and mind your own business, traitor."

If they tortured me, would I break? When they jerked her forward, she let go of the breath she hadn't realized she'd been holding. Torment and the doom of her mortality weren't her stop today. She was to linger here. A quick death could be a mercy, but she wasn't ready to die.

"We're not even wasting the time of our examiner to take you in there," said the shorter one. "You're to be sacrificed."

The little sunlight that managed to seep through the vents to the subterranean dungeon faded as they dragged her deeper into the tunnel. Shaalon shivered. Her captors led her through the stone caverns below the palace, which sat on the only mountain on Xerra.

The imposing structure had been carved out of the mountain side. The dungeon had been mined out of solid granite.

Water seeped through cracks in the small fractures in the rock surfaces. Escape was her one desperate thought as she searched the damp walls for any weapon. Her window of opportunity narrowed with each passing step.

A large metal door loomed ahead. She knew without being told it was *his* door. She'd heard of this. The prisoner must have held a high rank to have been offered a final request. Her captors tugged her along until the guard on her right stopped. The shorter one kept going, and her arm yanked painfully in its socket.

"What?" asked the one who'd kept walking. His beady eyes narrowed. "Let's get this over with."

"Don't you remember the last time?" the shorter one grimaced.

"How could I forget? But we won't let that happen again."

Shaalon's heart gave a quick pulse of pain as fear pumped through her veins.

"I won't go in first. Let's just push the woman inside and be done with it."

"Our orders are to watch him kill her."

"Her fate is sealed. What good will it do to see her torn apart? His kind only knows death. He wants revenge, or he'd never have made this his last request."

Nodding, the one on her left let go of a long sigh as he glanced between his partner and the door. "I'm no coward, but I'm also no fool. If he grabs one of us, we don't have an entire patrol to stop him. He killed four last time. The two of us would be quick work for a warrior."

A warrior. They weren't all killers, at least that's

what her father always said. They were once revered heroes from the best families. They were once the most feared and respected men of her world. Now they were criminals.

The shorter one cleared his throat. "I have a family."

The other nodded. "As do I. It's settled then. We shove the woman inside and let the beast have his last kill -- but it won't be us."

An angry cry echoed through the narrow passage, coming from whoever was behind the door and making her knees weak. Her guard yanked her up, or she'd have crumbled. They both looked at Shaalon, and she stared at the door. It might be the last thing she ever saw.

* * *

Cayylen paced in his cell. He had to get out before they executed him. Cayylen, son of Braxxon, the Duke of Miin, serving a death sentence. The notion was more than he could fathom. He was the heir to the wealthiest region of Xerra, but that wouldn't save him. He'd been caught in the middle of training. The punishment for warriors passing down their skills was an immediate death sentence for both the master and the apprentice. He'd been teaching his nephew the way. Strength ran deep in the roots of his family tree. He'd seen the traits in the boy from an early age, so when he was approached, he couldn't turn his blood away to find another teacher.

Cayylen prayed to the gods that Hexxer still lived. Anger filled him with a white-hot rage that blinded him. One day the warriors would rise again to restore the true religion to Xerra. The pretender on the throne would enjoy no mercy as his life ebbed under a warrior's blade. *Hopefully mine.* Cayylen slammed his fist against the stone wall and raged until his throat hurt.

He wasn't ready to die, but being trapped here was its own kind of death. "I wish they'd hurry and get it over with," Cayylen mumbled to himself. He leaned against the cold stone; his head hung low, his soul mired in despair. And then the door opened.

A woman came tumbling into the cell to land on the rough stone floor, crying out in pain. The door slammed shut. The terrified woman peered up at him through her long brown hair. Loose hair meant she was either a prostitute or a woman who'd just married.

Judging from her short, sleeveless dress, she was a new bride. Purple. She wore the color of his house, but she was not of his people. Her lighter skin and golden brown hair marked her as laborer class. Long ago her people had been bred to be subservient, hardy workers for the upper classes and warriors. The practice stopped long ago, but there was still a stigma associated with her ancestry even though those of laborer descent outnumbered everyone else on Xerra three-to-one.

Confusion and anger bubbled in him. He could handle death for his beliefs, but not mockery. The woman appeared terrified. Her big brown eyes were huge and very prominent in her small, regal features. He'd never seen a woman who was so beautiful in such a simple way. It had been far too long since he'd had a woman under him.

Cayylen's eyes narrowed as he pierced her with his gaze. "Who are you? What are you doing here?"

She gasped, rolled on her side, and curled into a ball.

Then he remembered his flippant last request. He'd asked to be given the daughter of his enemy. But this woman was no enemy. "Damn the gods!" This girl was meant for him to enjoy, but he was no rapist.

She shook. He saw her damaged knees bleeding and something twisted inside him. A connection hung between them. Maybe it was just that they were captive here together, or maybe it was...

He refused to let his mind speculate over a Soul Union. He had no male he'd be willing to share a bride with, so the revered Soul Trinity was never going to be his. Soul Union was far rarer, and the impossible odds of finding his mate here, while he awaited death, was laughable. Something protective rose up inside of him and made him angry at himself for putting her here with him. He had never thought for a moment they would give him a woman when he'd made the flippant request.

"Who are you?" he repeated.

"Please don't kill me," she whimpered. Tears ran unchecked down her cheeks, and he had the strangest urge to wipe them away.

"Do I have a reason to kill you? What have you done?"

She paled. His words had the desired effect, and she stopped crying. "I -- nothing. They've sentenced me to death, and you are to be my executioner."

Cayylen loosed a long string of curses under his breath. These idiots believed the rhetoric about warriors becoming bloodthirsty maniacs. Lies were told to children to profane the glorious past and prevent the young from seeking out the once illustrious ranks of the Warrior's Guild, Protectors of Xerra.

Cayylen crossed his arms over his chest. "Do you believe I will kill you?" He took a step toward her.

She scrambled away until her back hit the wall

opposite him. "Yes."

He imagined what he must look like to her. He stood twice her size and bare-chested. Men no longer honed their muscles as the warriors did. In only two generations, society had made his guild monsters. Stories of how they sacrificed babies to achieve immortality and a change of cultural attitude toward polyamory contributed to the spreading of falsehoods.

"Why? Have you ever met a warrior?"

"No. Warriors haven't been around since my father was young, not since the war. They're gone, all but you."

A slow smile spread across his face. She'd been sent to gather information on where his brothers hid. If they thought he'd trade his honor for sex, they were wrong. He would trust no woman, not even one this beautiful, that far. "I'm very much here. I'm not telling you anything, sweet spy. It was very crafty of them to dress you like a new bride of my clan."

She looked down at herself as if seeing her clothing for the first time. "Is that why they made me wear this? I -- I thought... They kept saying I was to satisfy the beast's appetite. Oh!" Her cheeks grew crimson. He could see she realized they'd meant sexual hunger because she pulled her legs closer to her body.

"I have never raped a woman. I do not plan to start with you, little bride. What crime brought you to me?"

She covered her face with her hands and wouldn't look at him. "You'll put a spell on me."

He chuckled. If either of them was weaving a spell, it was her. He couldn't stop looking at her. It was true that his kind was different. Warriors were blessed by the gods. But they'd never hurt an innocent. Drinking from the Mother's Spring gave them a long life and healed them from all but death. "How can I convince you of your safety, little bride?"

She peeked up at him. "Why would they bring me to my execution and leave me here if I'm safe?"

"Because they are fools who have been fed propaganda against me and my brothers since the cradle. I will not kill you. What earned you your death?"

"I tried to stop one of the king's guard from killing a pregnant woman protesting for her husband's release. I don't know what god she worships and I don't care."

He snorted out a gruff breath. "You are one of those, are you?"

"What do you mean by that?"

Cayylen grinned. She scowled, but her posture relaxed. His teasing drew her away from her unnecessary fear. "Those who believe all can coexist in this small land are fools. Everyone believes they pray to the true gods. Even brave little brides."

"Stop calling me that! My name is Shaalon."

"Ah, the word for beauty in the ancient tongue. Your parents made a good choice. You are very beautiful."

Another flush spread over Shaalon's cheeks and down her chest. Her fair skin colored nicely and he wondered how that skin would react to a suckling kiss. His love marks could last for days, branding her as his. *Where are these thoughts coming from?* His traitorous cock rose, and he shifted uncomfortably, hoping she didn't notice. He was not an animal. He would never force her.

He took a step back and felt the stone wall. They were as far apart as the tiny dome of rock allowed. "I am Cayylen." He had no idea why he gave her his name, but he did.

"Cayylen."

On her lips, his name sounded musical. His cock grew painfully hard in his tight leather pants. He groaned and shifted his weight, unable to sit in his current state, so he crossed his arms over his chest again and stayed there, looking down at her, which did nothing to end his erection.

"What do we do?" Shaalon whispered.

He could only think of one activity he had any interest in and he doubted she would spread her legs for him, so he remained silent.

* * *

"Seriously, what are we going to do?" Shaalon asked.

"Fuck. Fuck hard until they put us to death," he said without a hint of emotion.

She gasped. Glaring she shook her head. "I thought the Mother frowned on that sort of thing."

He chuckled. "Most gods do." Cayylen ran his hand through his dark hair. "But the Mother understands all things. She accepts the carnal needs of her children as long as they never abandon their own children. She only frowns on those who scatter their seed heedlessly. We won't be alive long enough to be concerned with that."

"Do you have a plan to escape? Aren't warriors supposed to have magic on their side?"

"You have heard of our talents, not just our blood lust?"

Heat warmed her cheeks, and she glared at him. In another time and place, she'd have been taken to his bed and loved until the sunrise. She'd have enjoyed respect for being with him. A child born from the union with a warrior was a cause for the greatest celebration, and rare, but now they were hidden away so they wouldn't be killed. If they survived this and she became pregnant, she'd have to hide their child's paternity. His time was over in all ways. He had nothing to offer this beauty, except pleasure.

Shaalon gazed up at him with a strange mixture of awe and desire in her expression. "Ye -- yes. I've heard a true warrior is powerful, but believes in justice. Those men are gone. The warriors became vicious killers, and that is why the king had them rounded up and executed. How did you escape? Where have you hidden for so long?"

"How do you know I'm not a young man -- a new generation?"

Shaalon stood. "I know they don't train warriors anymore, and your eyes are the eyes of a man who has lived his lifetime, but your body is..." She flushed. "Your body is not the body of an old man."

Cayylen grinned. Beautiful and intelligent. "I was born before your grandparents. You're right. I'm not a young man."

She moved, almost as if she wanted to touch him, and then dropped her hand. "But you hold so much vitality. It is some kind of magic."

"It's not magic. It's religion. The Mother cares for her true followers and their families. The Mother's Milk nourishes my youth."

"I see why the warriors are so feared. No mortal man could stand against your Brotherhood."

He nodded. She was right, those that didn't follow the ways of The Mother would never defeat a warrior. The king feared them, and because he feared them, he turned the people against them. "If we are to die, let us enjoy one last freedom. Let me love your body."

Her mouth fell open. He had shocked the innocent little bride. He could see the rejection in her eyes.

"Ye -- Yes. Show me what it is to have a real warrior in my bed. Make love to me."

Now it was his turn to be shocked. She wanted to say no, he'd seen it, but she'd proven her courage. She was a fitting tribute for him.

Cayylen moved toward her before she could change her mind and took her in his arms. She gasped, and he grinned as he pressed his lips to hers. Her eyes fluttered closed. He laid her down on the cell floor. In another lifetime he'd have taken her in his massive bed, plush with pillows, and prepared for their union. This was far from ideal, but he'd never wanted a woman more than he wanted this one.

Chapter Two

Shaalon took a deep breath, let it out slowly, and decided to trust him.

Cayylen cradled her head as he lay her back on the cold, unyielding rock floor. There was nothing soft here, nothing warm. He was the only heat warming her, his muscular body looming over her. He was so big. Turning her head to the side, she closed her eyes. She'd heard the first time hurt and she tensed, waiting for some unknown agony. Holding her breath, she slowly relaxed when the pain never came. She opened her eyes and cautiously turned to look into his beautiful brown eyes. His broad chest heaved with each uneven breath he took. He fixed his gaze on her with an intensity that stole her ability to think. He ran his hand down her shoulder, baring it. She gasped. This male wanted her, and the knowledge was euphoric. His knuckles brushed her cheek gently. It was strange that such a mass of sinew and muscle was capable of tenderness. Her breath came out in little pants.

"You stood up to the king's army. Do not let that courage fail you now." There was a husky dare in his tone. "I will not hurt you." Cayylen's sexy smile sent flutters through her stomach. She didn't trust herself to speak.

He brushed her lower lip with his thumb. "I have nothing to offer you, and we may both die tomorrow, but you're meant to be mine. You are special. I can't explain it, but you were sent from the Mother to comfort me. Let me show you how much pleasure you can feel."

Every fiber of her body wanted this man to claim her. She nodded. One small move said so much. His lips pressed to hers with a demanding force that left no quarter for gentleness. She moaned against the firm, confident pressure. His tongue slipped into her mouth, and she let hers dance with his in a primal rhythm. Some instinct pushed her to kiss him back with the same passion he gave her.

Cayylen's hand slipped under her dress and ran up her side. She trembled. His mouth pulled away from hers. He trailed kisses down her jawline until his lips were on her neck. The unkempt growth of stubble on his jaw tickled her.

She gasped as he cupped her breast. His breath fanned across her shoulder. He untied the belt around her waist with one hand and opened her thin dress to bare her completely. He was a virtual stranger, but for some reason she experienced no shame being naked before him. His touch was right. He calmed her soul in a way she wasn't able to explain.

Cayylen sat up. She didn't know what to do so she remained where she was. He pulled her to him, so she was on his lap, straddling him. The sleeves of her dress fell down her arms to lay rumpled on the stone floor. His large hands splayed across her back, and she faced him. He kissed her neck. The sensation tickled, but also caused feelings she'd never experienced before to bloom. A boldness she didn't know she had gripped her as she ran her hand over his shoulder and chest until she traced the defined muscles of his abdomen, and the sexy "V" just above his leather pants. He was overdressed. He sucked in sharply, and she grinned against his mouth. When he jerked a second time, she assumed he was ticklish, and she ran her fingertips over the same spot on his muscular stomach. He groaned.

His mouth went to her nipple reverently and

what he did with his tongue felt amazing. She closed her eyes and held his head to her breast. She managed not to fall off his lap, but the pleasure made her quiver. He sucked hard and her back arched. She wanted to protest as he laid her back on the floor, using her dress as a barrier between the cold rock and her skin.

* * *

Cayylen pushed the hair out of her eyes and off her forehead, pulling a few stray strands away from her mouth before kissing her again. Using his knee, he spread her thighs. She didn't resist. He ran his hand over his woman's hip. *My woman.* The thought took him by surprise and couldn't stop his smile, even as they kissed. Joy surged through him.

This was what he existed for -- Shaalon. Soul Union. There was no more denying the truth. A vibrant and wonderful excitement bloomed in his chest as his heart beat in time with hers. Why now? Why couldn't he have found her at a better time? His desire rushed into some dangerous territory. He wanted to live more than ever. He hadn't realized he'd given up until this moment.

She groaned and arched her back, writhing against him. Her pubis ground against his groin. Cayylen shuddered. He needed to maintain control, or he'd never be able to hold off his release.

In another life, he would have made her his in a way she would never be for another man. He'd have bound her soul to his. But he'd settle for the comfort her body had to offer him. "Do you want me, Shaalon?" He needed to hear the words.

She sat up a little, using her arm for support and tossed her head, making her long brown hair flow over her shoulders. She bit her lip. After a pause, she let go of a sigh. "Yes, more than anything." The raw vulnerability in her expression gripped him. "I shouldn't, but if I'm going to die I want to know what it's like to make love to a man like you before they end me. I want that one last rebellion."

He would protect her, somehow. His innocent rebel made his cock ache.

She arched her back and whimpered again, rubbing her pussy against his leg. Her eyes were veiled with the long black lashes, and a soft blush stained her high cheekbones. Even in the near darkness, his special eyesight let him see her wanton expression.

Cayylen's fingers ran down her soft skin, starting at the middle of her belly and then passing through her downy pubic hair until he found her wet heat. His fingers glided to her clitoris. She cried out and her hips jerked. He flicked her again. Lust hazed her half-closed eyes.

She reached up and put her arms around his neck. He let her pull him down to her mouth as he reached out and brushed her breast. He knelt beside her on the rock floor. Making love to her felt like praying. She was his miracle from the Mother, a goddess to worship, a woman to bind with for eternity. He'd had more life than was his due, but with her beside him, it wasn't enough. He wanted another lifetime with a gluttony that shocked him. When he was captured, he'd been tired of hiding, ready to give up, but a new energy filled him as she whimpered against his lips.

"I won't hurt you," Cayylen said softly. He pinched her nipple before sliding his hand down her stomach. She jerked and moaned as he continued to caress between her legs. She closed her eyes and threw back her head, her breathing heavy. She was close, but he wasn't ready to release her from her lust just yet.

When he lowered her to her back and took his hands away from her body, her lower lip trembled as she gazed up at him with uncertainty.

"Di -- did I do something wrong?"

"Never. You're doing everything right, perfect." He stood up and took off his pants. Now they were both naked. He knelt beside her and rubbed her cheek tenderly. She shut her eyes and leaned into his caress. The gesture made his heart do a funny little flip. When she opened her eyes, their gazes locked.

"I won't hurt you," Cayylen repeated, willing her to believe him. "Do you trust me?" He tweaked her nipple. She jerked and moaned. Cayylen's fingers dipped into the heat of her pussy. She closed her eyes and threw back her head. "Yes! Yes," she cried out. He rubbed her slick clit harder and faster.

She came, her mouth opened and a flush spread down her chest and over her pale breasts. Her hips bucked and he didn't let up until tears leaked from the corners of her eyes. He slowed his hand and gradually stopped as the sounds she made died down to a soft whimper.

Cayylen wrapped his arms around her and kissed her deeply. Shaalon clung to him and went limp in his arms. He rubbed her neck and shoulders. He was just getting started. He knew he would enjoy this, but he'd ensure she did, as well. Her pleasure was his responsibility. He liked to make sure his women came first, but this time her enjoyment filled him with joy that went beyond the promise of his own release. Her contentment nourished his spirit in a way he didn't know he needed. Making her come had been the most spiritual moment of his long life. When he stopped kissing her, she stayed sitting up, looking at him with a dazed expression.

"Rest on your back, beauty," Cayylen said. "Open for me."

Shaalon obeyed. She stared up at him with blind obedience.

She spread her legs widely, her body inviting him. Cayylen's heart soared. There was purity in her, and the absence of resistance suddenly struck him. *I don't deserve this gift. Oh Mother, make me worthy.* Gratitude overflowed in his heart. He caressed her slickness again and smiled at how ready she was for him. It had been so long since he'd been with a woman who knew what he was and still wanted him.

Shaalon was the most important woman in the universe. When he gazed into her face, he saw a potential for something more than mere existence. Her simple submission was the most beautiful thing he'd ever witnessed. He couldn't stop the Soul Union forming between them. Cayylen doomed her the same moment she saved him.

"I want to taste you. May I?" Cayylen asked.

She appeared confused.

"I want to put my mouth where my hand is." Cayylen gave her clit a quick pinch.

A flicker of fear and embarrassment crossed her face, but she nodded yes. Cayylen moved so that he knelt between her legs. Softly, he placed his mouth on her intimate lips. She jerked.

He reached out and stroked her arm. "It's all right, beauty. I'll make you feel good." He returned to the work of loving her with his mouth. This time she only flinched a little, but her body remained rigid. He continued to suck and lick until the tension began leaving her. Then she made a soft noise that turned into a whimper.

Shaalon moaned, grinding her pussy against his

mouth. Her genuine response was all the permission he needed to enjoy her. He loved her tenderly, but he didn't hold back as he sucked her clit into his mouth -- hard. She bucked, making unintelligible sounds. He didn't relent. Lapping at her labia, he moved to flick her clit again. He plunged his tongue inside of her and then wiggled it in and out, fucking her, worshiping her with his tongue. She turned her head to the side and grasped his hair, pulling him closer. Replacing his tongue with two fingers, he wiggled them inside of her as he continued his efforts on her clitoris.

"Please!" she cried. Her simple plea resounded in the small space. Confusion saturated her tone. Cayylen knew she was calling for cock without realizing what she really needed. That naiveté made this so much better. He was teaching her what her body wanted. Her desire was clay for him to shape and he wanted her lust to become art.

This time he wouldn't give her release so easily. He pulled back, and she let out a surprised gasp. "Don't stop," she begged.

Cayylen grinned. "I'm just getting started, little bride."

"Started? There's more?"

"Much more." His smile broadened. "Explore me."

She worried her lower lip between her teeth. "What do you mean?"

"Touch me. Anywhere. Everywhere."

Her eyes lit up as she reached out cautiously. She'd touched him earlier, instinctually, but now he saw she thought about her actions and that changed her confidence. Now she touched lighter, uncertain. She grazed his defined pecs, and he snared her hand, pressing her fingertips firmly against his skin.

"Touch me," he commanded.

Shaalon trailed her fingers down his chest and wrapped them around his cock. She stroked him, and her curious exploration left him on the verge of release.

Cayylen's soul cracked as Shaalon slipped inside his heart to fill a deep hole. He hadn't experienced the emptiness in its entirety until she warmed him. He held her head gently and gazed into her face so he could memorize the way she appeared at this very moment

He groaned. "Today my soul will unite with yours. Do you have the courage to belong to me?"

* * *

Belong to me. Shaalon tightened her grip just a little. She understood this was something deeper than sex, but she was willing to give him anything he asked. She was his completely. "Yes."

He sucked in a breath and let it out with a groan which sounded almost like a sigh as his breath fanned against her breast. She hissed through her teeth as he leaned down to draw her nipple between his lips. He sucked hard as she stroked his cock. He switched sides and loved her right bud, and she gripped him harder, exploring the velvet skin over his hardness. He groaned again. Cayylen's response to her touch ignited her daring as she rubbed up and down the length of him faster.

He nibbled against her breast, causing a long breathy, sensual sigh. One of her hands tangled in his dark brown hair while the other stroked him. When her fingers moved to cup his sac, he released her nipple. The cool air swirled around the place he'd vacated like an invisible caress. Shaalon bit her lip to keep her moan from escaping. Even in the darkness, she could see his eyes and the smoldering look he gave her only made her wetter.

"What if the guards hear us?" Shaalon whispered, dropping her hand. "I -- I'm scared I'll make too much noise. What I'm feeling is so -- I can't even put it into words."

"You deserve better than this," he raged against her ear before kissing her neck.

"Nothing could be better than this," she retorted. "I want more."

She didn't resist as he moved lower on her body and parted her thighs again, dropping a kiss just under her navel before his head dipped between her legs. His rough tongue slowly loved her clitoris. The sensation made her hips jerk. She was sensitive from his previous attention, and she closed her eyes as the heat built hotter and faster this time. He clasped onto her sides, and he held her, his strokes becoming a rapid assault of sensation. Her body responded to him in a mindless joy. A track of moisture ran down her ass, making her squirm.

Cayylen held her firmly. Everything about this should be wrong, but the crazy part was she didn't care. She needed this release, but most of all she needed him. She whimpered. She wanted something. Her body was ready for something. But she couldn't name that vague need.

She moaned and arched her back. "I want… inside… me. Please!" Shaalon cried out.

He pulled her leg up so her knee was against his hip and her legs were wide for him. "And now we become one," he said as his cock found her ready entrance. She gasped with surprise as he slipped inside of her with a single very manly thrust and pleasured grunt. There was almost no pain, he entered her so swiftly. She gasped at the perfect fullness.

He stilled, his body joined with hers. "It will be good again soon."

Cayylen found her clit, and he strummed her desire back to life. She closed her eyes and let herself stop thinking. Her hands found his ass, and she squeezed his perfection. He thrust with even, fast strokes. His finger managed to strum her clit even as he drove hard. Her back arched again, and she gasped. Opening her eyes, she looked up at the uneven stone ceiling as she came.

"Cayylen!" The cry left her lips before she could stop it. She lowered her gaze from the rock above them to look into his big brown eyes. He stilled, but their bodies were still locked together.

"I love you Shaalon; I swear I do. I feel Soul Unity with you. I can't understand how this happened, but I loved you the moment I saw you."

He kissed her before she could protest. Her eyes fluttered closed as she kissed him back and emotion burst through her. He moved in her again, throwing his head back. His face was a mask of strain. She fought the urge to scream by pressing her lips against his shoulder. Orgasm rippled through her body, mind, and spirit. He had his face pressed in her hair. A kaleidoscope of color exploded behind her eyelids. Shaalon shook with the force of her release. Her body responded to him without her conscious decision. She rocked against him, sliding him deeper inside of her. The beautiful friction caused intense wails of joy to erupt from her throat unhindered.

Shaalon squeezed her eyes closed and let her body become mindless sensation. Every single stroke of his cock brought a fresh spasm of pleasure through her. He was thrusting hard and fast, and his cock stroked her clit with his every move. The only sounds escaping her were little whimpers of pleasure. Shaalon opened her eyes and gazed up at Cayylen. His face twisted into a mask of concentration as he pumped inside of her. She closed her eyes and arched her back as Cayylen drove deeper.

The pleasure didn't ebb. The physical joy continued as the seconds became timeless. Nothing mattered but this man and his cock. A keening wail left her throat, and her breath hitched as she hit the zenith of her pleasure and she came so hard she saw sparks behind her closed eyelids. Nothing in her whole experience prepared her for this nirvana of orgasm. Her mind floated disconnectedly as her body indulged in the sinful consummation of mating.

When he came, he let loose a long groan, and the heat of his release filled her. They clung to each other.

Chapter Three

Cayylen leaned down and peppered Shaalon with kisses, lingering on her lips, before pulling back to look at her face. He took both her breasts into his hands and rolled her nipples gently between his thumb and fingers. She gasped. The sound was music to his ears. Making love to her was what he'd been born to do. He felt her in every cell in his body. She was a part of him now.

Instead of quenching his need, their orgasms had only whetted his hunger for more of her.

She peeked at him from beneath her long lashes, and her head rested on his left forearm. He stroked her face, breasts, and stomach with his right hand in lazy seduction. His hands roamed her restlessly as he gazed deeply into her eyes. She regarded him with complete adoration. The Soul Union was so strong he could hear her thoughts.

"I want to cherish you," Cayylen whispered. "May I love you again?

"Yes. Oh yes."

He moaned as he crushed her to him. Hot and demanding, his lips burned hers with need. His erection pressed against her thigh, and all Shaalon could do was cling to him with desperate want.

Cayylen could smell her lust. He inhaled deeply. Shaalon's natural perfume infused the air with a heady combination of wet pussy and pheromones. He broke the kiss and positioned her on her hands and knees in front of him. Then he stroked her clit until she moaned.

"More. Please," she whimpered.

"Is this what you want, beauty?" Cayylen asked as he grabbed her hips, pulling her to him. His nostrils flared. Her scent filled his lungs.

"Yes. Oh, yes," she gasped.

The soft plea filled his ears. Each syllable rang as if sweet music. His breathing sped up. Sweat beaded his chest. His balls ached with a need so great he feared he'd never be able to give her what she needed. "I'm going to take you again. Tell me now if this is too soon."

"It's not soon enough." She breathed the words huskily.

Cayylen chuckled. "I love you. Tell me you're mine."

She nodded, turning to glance back at him. "I'm yours." Her expression was earnest and innocent. She was pure desire -- the embodiment of sex -- and he wanted to enjoy everything she had to offer.

A surge of protectiveness rose inside of him. The sight of her lithe body was the most erotic thing he'd ever witnessed. He caressed the soft skin on her perfect bum. She wore her nudity gloriously.

"Mine," he whispered as he leaned over her. His muscles rippled as he fought back the desire to plunge inside of her heedlessly. "I can smell how much you want me." He uttered the words with reverence as he placed a kiss on her back before plunging his cock inside her ready pussy. He held her hips as he took her. With every thrust, his body fit hers perfectly, and he fought back his release.

"I'm so close," she murmured. "I'm -- it's good, so good."

"Let go. Come for me."

He pumped into her harder. Shaalon cried out. He wrapped her hair around his hand and pulled her head back to kiss her neck. She wailed wordless grunts with the force of her orgasm. The indescribable strength of this carnality thrilled him. She was everything.

Cayylen jerked and growled her name tenderly. His mouth remained pressed to her throat as her muscles gripped his cock, milking him of his seed. Cayylen put his arms around her and held her to him. He rested his head against her back, her ass pressed tight against him. They stayed like that for an infinite moment. She remained resting on her forearms and knees. The only sound in the room was their hard breathing.

* * *

Cayylen kissed her shoulder. "Did I hurt you?" he asked softly. "It hasn't been long since you gave me the gift of your virginity. I wanted to wait longer, but I couldn't resist you."

"It -- everything felt right. You didn't do anything that I didn't enjoy."

"This thing between us is more powerful than love. Your body -- your soul -- recognizes that you belong to me. I'm going to keep you safe. I don't know how, but I swear it," Cayylen promised with passionate conviction. He turned her so that she lay in his arms and he gazed into her eyes, marveling at her beauty. The truth in his tone filled her with unexpected peace. "The Mother is laughing at us. Her timing is far from kind. If I can save you I will. I just want to hold you. If today is my last, at least we have this moment."

Shaalon gave him a half smile. "If only we could make a moment last forever."

"One moment with you is worth a lifetime with anyone else." Cayylen kissed her forehead. "I just want to hold you."

He was right, and she wanted his arms around her too, but she just couldn't tell him because her throat closed painfully tight as emotion choked her.

Cayylen kissed her neck. "Are you afraid? I will not give up on seeing you freed. I would not leave you behind."

"I trust you." Shaalon sighed the words as she gazed into his eyes. And she did. Somehow laying in his arms made her feel safe even in this prison awaiting death. Exhaustion caught up with her, and she blinked, willing her eyes to remain fixed on his. Sleep won as her eyes fluttered closed and his arms tightened around her.

* * *

Looking at his woman filled Cayylen with both exhilaration and terror. He tenderly pushed the strands of dark hair off her cheek with the pad of his index finger. She didn't stir. He grinned in the darkness. He'd worn her out. A sense of pride mingled with an infinite sadness pulling him from joy into despair. His role should be her protector, but he was helpless. Bitter anger rolled through him and his teeth clenched. He watched her sleep and knew he'd do everything in his power to free them. She was all that mattered. "I would die for you," Cayylen whispered.

She drew in a soft breath and moved closer to him, drawn to him even in sleep. The bond between them was palpable as he felt her contentment. Even with death looming near she trusted him. Her posture remained relaxed, and her cheek rested against his forearm, beautiful in her repose. A small amount of light filtered in from a spidering crack in the rock just above the door. He wanted to see her in the sun and make love to her under the stars. Watching her execution was far more likely, and he tightened his hold on her, which caused her to mumble and groan in her sleep.

A crack in the rock... He gazed up at the minor

defect. Stories of the power Soul Union gave a warrior nagged in his memory. If he could crack the wall further, it would run right down to where the bolts held the door in the rock. He looked at his sleeping woman. If he got her out of here, he'd make her his bride with the full ceremony. Warriors needed to find their soul brides. They needed that strength to fight for the right to exist. He'd fight because he had a reason now. The time for hiding was done.

He kissed her, and she stretched her eyes blinking open. "What is it?" she whispered, yawning.

He stroked her cheek. "If I told you the love you've given me has made me strong -- stronger than a normal man -- would you believe me?"

Shaalon nodded mutely. The pure trust in her gaze humbled him. More determined than ever, he looked at the crack in the wall and willed the tales of Soul Union to prove true.

Cayylen stood, and then pulled on his pants. "You'd better get dressed."

He felt the weight of his woman's gaze on him. He watched her pull her dress on out of the corner of his eye. The responsibility to her hit him like a fist and the urge to protect what was his rose up without warning. Failing her wasn't an option. He walked over to the door and slammed his fist against the stone under the crack. Nothing out of the ordinary happened. He pounded again, and this time the door rattled.

A loud bang on the opposite side of the door made him pause. Laughter followed, and Cayylen glared at the metal. "Are you finished with her? Your time is up."

The door opened. Cayylen gave no thought to his nudity as he rushed the guards, but there were more of them than they'd brought the last time. He fought against the bastards, but they were strong and better prepared. They all wore protective gear and held stun rope which was an electrified cord used to incapacitate and bind prisoners. He fought against their hold as two of them cornered Shaalon. She was still naked too. Her terrified gaze met his, and he willed her to be strong.

"I will find you." Cayylen struggled harder.

One of the guards tightened the stun rope. "You'll find her corpse." He chuckled. "Right before we make you one."

He'd never felt as helpless as he did the moment they took her out of the cell and he lost sight of her. "If you hurt her I'll make sure your deaths are miserable."

The guards were a little cockier as he remained subdued. "Are you a warrior or a woman?" The shortest one quipped. "I say, woman."

Cayylen's anger seethed. "Better a woman than a snub-nosed little man like you." His retort earned him a lash to the cheek with the end of the stun rope. The guards backed out of the cell and released him with a shove as they slammed the heavy door.

Rage burst from him, and he threw back his head and let the hatred echo against the stone around him. Something deep erupted with his cry, something strong. He could see down the narrow corridor and feel the pinching, intrusive hands on her body as if he were Shaalon. Her terror was palpable. The bond resonated her experience, and he lived every moment of her agony. The sensation spurred him on to save her. He had to keep her from suffering further. Everything inside of him demanded he stop what was happening. She belonged to him, and these men wouldn't take her away without a fight.

Cayylen didn't think or plan, he just acted. This

time, when he slammed his fist against the stone, the wall shook and debris scattered down. The fissure grew as the top widened and the crack ran farther down the wall. Hammering with all his pent-up fury, he didn't let up his assault. Broken chunks fell, and the sound of the rock splitting thundered in his ears. When the granite cracked around the door frame, he had a jolt of confidence and a boost of strength.

The metal of the door groaned under the weight of the collapsing rock, and Cayylen pushed hard against the barrier until it gave with a crash. And then he was running. Instinct led him down twists and turns. He didn't think to save himself; she was all he cared about. Running until he saw the group of men, he paused as his wrath built. They handled Shaalon roughly, and the sight only fueled the power growing inside of him.

Cayylen embraced the power as he let the Soul Union take over. He rushed at the men, unconcerned that he was outnumbered six to one, grabbing the closest one around the neck and slamming him against the wall. The group turned, shock etched on their faces. For a moment, none of them moved, and then the spell was broken. The relief and love on Shaalon's face touched him, but he only had a split second to consider her reaction before the fray began in earnest.

Cayylen grabbed the first man he reached and broke his neck in a single motion, letting the body crumple thoughtlessly and taking hold of the next man. He dispatched two more the same way as he'd ended the first man's life. The injuries inflicted on him didn't even slow him down as he worked his way through the group, killing with a mindless need to remove the threat to his woman.

The king's men drew weapons. With his bare

hands, he disarmed one and then another. He broke the neck of the man who'd tried to insult him earlier and took the laser rifle out of the dead man's hand. He shot another. He saw one of the men run off, dragging Shaalon with him. Cayylen slammed the last two men against the wall, knocking them unconscious before running after the one foolish enough to take his woman hostage.

The man reached the end of the corridor and turned, holding his weapon to Shaalon's temple. "Stay away, or I'll kill her!"

Cayylen stopped moving. This enemy held every ounce of Cayylen's future happiness in his hands. His precious little bride stood stiffly, silently pleading with her eyes as she gazed at him. Uncertain of his next move, he sized up his opponent. Cowards were dangerous, and this one stank of fear. Shifty eyes and a twitching lip told Cayylen he couldn't trust the man to let Shaalon go, even if he put down his weapon. There had to be another way to secure her safety.

She struggled against her captor's hold. Fear made him indecisive. He'd never been afraid in a battle, until now. For the first time, he had something to lose. Soul Trinity made sense to him now. The idea that her security was his sole responsibility weighed heavy on him as he stood there unsure of his next move.

A crash made his thoughts go blank, and the wall beside them exploded. The guard and Shaalon were knocked into the opposite wall, hard. Too hard.

Cayylen coughed. "Shaalon!" He coughed again. "Shaalon!" No response.

Without taking the time to assess the danger of what had destroyed the rock wall he stumbled toward the pile of rubble where he'd seen her body crumple.

She lay under a large chunk of granite, unmoving. Luckily, a pile of debris kept the heavy weight from crushing her. Tossing the boulder away he picked her up. Her head was bleeding profusely, but her chest rose and fell. He let go of the breath he'd been holding as he assured himself she was alive. Relief mingled with his fear. They weren't safe yet, not even close, but at least they were together. One threat at a time. He turned, using his body to shield her as he peered into the hole in the cavern. Whatever was coming would not touch her. He'd die to keep her safe.

"You and your troubles. When are you going to learn to stay away from the king's guard?" Prince Rexxon stepped out of the gap.

Cayylen's hope soared. "How did you find me?"

"I said a prayer to the Mother," Rexxon said, grinning. "And we followed the energy signature of your weapon. The idiots didn't bother to destroy your laser pistol. I built it myself, so it wasn't a challenge to trace the unique energy reading."

"We? Tavvor isn't with your woman?" They were in a Soul Trinity with an Earth woman.

"No. He's with Alexa, but I brought Jakkon with me."

The giant male, Jakkon, stepped out of the damaged area as well. The big man's scarred face and massive body would strike fear in the hearts of their enemies. The warrior had kind eyes, but in a battle, they turned cold. He was one of the few men Cayylen trusted at his side.

Both of his friends grinned as if they were having a social visit. These were warriors from the old days. He'd fought many battles with these men, and they'd saved each other's lives. They'd come to his aid yet again. "I'm glad to see you both."

"And I see you have your hands full." Rexxon pointed to Shaalon. Then his expression turned serious. "We should get her to a healer."

"Yes." Cayylen agreed. "But getting out of here is our first challenge."

Rexxon motioned toward the hole in the wall. "Come on. We'll get you and your woman to The Haven, brother."

They ran through the tunnel created by the explosion. The temperature immediately dropped as they ran through the jagged rock and darkness enveloped them. Drawing on his warrior training, Cayylen navigated the passage without stumbling while holding Shaalon tight. He worried the space might collapse around them. The sound of his warrior brethren ahead gave him the confidence to take his woman into the unknown. Yesterday, he wouldn't have given traversing this path a second thought. Today, he had every reason in the world for caution. The life he held in his arms was more precious to him than his own. He realized he'd need a soul trinity or he'd never have another moment without worry.

A light ahead made him run faster. Freedom. They'd almost made it. He could see the sun glinting off the crystal of the palace. Pushing himself harder, he held Shaalon tightly. Pain stung his cheek as the whiz of a laser bullet told him they weren't safe yet. Shouting guards were behind them. Another shot hurtled past him. He jerked as agony tore through his shoulder and almost dropped his woman.

Fear. He wasn't afraid for himself, but for his soul bride. If he failed, they'd both die. Her death wasn't an option.

Rexxon motioned from the lift gate of a ship. The small craft was new and displayed the insignia of

Zayyrin, the leader of the warriors. *War.* The existence of this ship shouted for the long overdue fight, but now that he'd found the other half of his soul the joy this battle should give him wasn't in his heart.

Cayylen took a running jump and landed on the lift. His feet clanged against the metal, and the sound reverberated in the massive hole where their escape vessel sat. His brothers had blown a hole through the center of the palace garden and then through the rocky ground to get to the dungeon. Zayyrin had clearly spared no expense when he'd commissioned this craft and Cayylen suspected he was using this rescue to send a message.

As soon as Cayylen was inside, the lift rose and closed. Shaalon was still unconscious. He couldn't lose her. Looking around, he spied the medical kit on the wall. He needed to scan her to determine the extent of her injuries. Rexxon sat down in the co-pilot's seat.

Jakkon's fingers flew over the controls. "Buckle up."

Assessing her condition would have to wait. Jakkon's tone was grim. Cayylen strapped his woman into her seat and then took the one next to her. He hadn't even snapped his harness into place when the ship shot straight up so fast it made his stomach lurch.

Jakkon flipped some switches above his head, and the ship veered sharply right. The comm crackled.

"You aren't destroying my ship, are you?" Zayyrin's deep baritone voice was unmistakable.

"I'm just seeing what she can do. We have him, and he brought a friend," Jakkon said.

"Oh?"

"He's taken the plunge and found Soul Unity."

Zayyrin laughed. "Only Cayylen would go in a prisoner and come out in a Soul Union! I hope she's prepared to stand by his side during this war."

Jakkon glanced back at Cayylen, then looked at Shaalon. "I'm sure any woman who'd bond with him will be. But she's hurt."

"Bring her home. We'll take care of her in The Haven." Zayyrin's words sent a wave of relief through Cayylen. If their leader had denied her sanctuary, he would have even less to offer her. At least he had a home and a cause to give his bride.

The comm crackled as the connection terminated. Rexxon unbuckled and went for the medical kit. He stumbled as the ship took a hard left. "We might not have safety on the planet, but we've managed to keep The Haven hidden on the dark side of The Mother's moon."

A fitting place for them to find sanctuary. The smallest moon was the last place the king would expect them to be building their sky armada. There would be no more hiding. The king would be out for blood. He'd been drinking Mother's Milk for years, and even though his life was unnaturally long, he hadn't followed the religious practices that kept the warriors young. His mental health had declined, and as his body failed him he became more dangerous and unpredictable.

Rexxon knelt next to Shaalon and opened the medical kit. He fumbled with the scanner. "I've never been good with these things."

"Here." Cayylen took the device. He depressed the button for several seconds, until the light flashed red. Another press and then it flashed green. "If we make it off the planet in one piece I'll be happy." He slowly waved the device over his woman, and the indicator bleeped.

"We'll make it. It's winning the war I'll be happy

about. Fighting that tyrant is long overdue."

Nodding, Cayylen scanned Shaalon a second time. "Zayyrin is the greatest of us. With him leading us we'll win."

"I agree. We will." Jakkon laughed as he gave his input. "But this is not the time to be taking a mate alone. You are a brave man to take a woman without a second in times like these. Judging from the circumstances you found her in, you'll need all the help you can get."

Chapter Four

Cayylen frowned. The scanner indicated Shaalon had a concussion, but was otherwise fine. He worried because she wasn't waking up. He ran his hand through his hair and sighed. Jakkon continued to navigate them away from the inferior pilots in the king's army. He couldn't believe they were having this conversation while fleeing for their lives. "Brother, this wasn't planned."

Jakkon glanced back, smiling. "The greatest loves never are."

"Focus on keeping our asses from being blown to atoms," Rexxon growled.

Jakkon muttered under his breath as he turned around. Cayylen recognized the English curse words.

Rexxon chuckled. "Did your wife teach you to swear like that?"

"My wife could…"

A rumble on the starboard side cut Jakkon short. The smell of smoke made Cayylen's heart beat quicken. The sound of the safety systems activating to put out the fire was a relief.

"We're hit, but I think we're okay to take her off world." Jakkon worked with practiced fingers as he slid the navigation controls around on the dash screen. The lights in the cabin turned a dim green. "I'm diverting what energy I can to the thrusters. Don't worry. I'm not cutting the life support, not even what Rexxon is breathing."

"Funny. Seriously, is there anything we can do to help?" Rexxon asked.

"Just keep Cayylen's woman alive and hold on tight." Jakkon slammed his thumb down on the screen. "You might want to buckle up now."

Rexxon hurried to his seat and the moment his harness clicked into place Jakkon pulled his hand back. They were all thrown back against their seats as the g-force hit them hard. Cayylen reached out and took Shaalon's hand. Even unconscious he wanted her to feel his love and concern.

They weren't hit again, and the vessel left the atmosphere without incident. Nothing the king had could match this new technology. Cayylen had never seen anything like this ship. He let go of the breath he'd been unconsciously holding.

"Whooo!" Rexxon slapped his hands together. "I could kiss you, brother. I won't, but I could."

Jakkon laughed. "Kiss Zayyrin, it's his amazing ship. I'm just the pilot."

"And a hell of a good one you are," Rexxon said. "That was some amazing flying."

Shaalon moaned, and Cayylen focused on her. She blinked. "What -- what happened?"

"We've escaped." Cayylen rescanned her. "You're on your way to The Haven. How are you feeling?"

"Like I was hit by a stone wall."

"Ceiling, actually." Rexxon turned to look at her. "I'm your man's brother warrior, Rexxon."

Their pilot glanced back. "I am Jakkon."

"Thank you for saving us." Shaalon gave both Rexxon and Jakkon pointed looks. "Where is The Haven?"

Rexxon grinned. "The dark side of our smallest moon."

"Space? We're going to space?" Shaalon gaped. "I've never been off world."

Cayylen noticed her shaking, and he put his hands over hers. "It'll be okay. Jakkon is a great pilot, and we know what we're doing. You're safe."

"But for how long? The king won't be forgiving, considering we blew up his dungeon."

"Only part of it," Jakkon said. "And to be fair you and Cayylen are innocent of the crime."

She smiled a cute, lopsided grin. "I don't know if that should make me feel better, but somehow it does. Thanks."

"My pleasure, sister." Jakkon glanced back at her. "Welcome to the warrior's guild. We've declared war today. Will you have the courage to support your husband?"

Her mouth fell open. "War?" Then she flushed. "Are we really married?"

Cayylen took her chin in his hand, and she looked into his eyes. "When we can, I will give you a proper ceremony, but we are bonded. I am yours, and you are mine. I promise to love you today and every day until I draw my last breath."

Her flush deepened, and a small smile cured her full lips.

"Your last breath may come sooner than you think, brother," Rexxon said. "This war has been a long time coming, and our battle is long overdue."

Shaalon frowned. "What the king has done isn't right, but is war the only answer?"

Cayylen squeezed her hand. "I understand your concern, but we have run out of choices."

Rexxon scowled. "War is the only answer left to us. The king has become a tyrant. He's unstable. Have you wondered how the man has lived to rule as many years as he has?"

"Well, yes, but..."

"But nothing," Rexxon interrupted. "He's been using the Mother's Milk to live, but because he's not one of us he doesn't truly understand how to use her life-giving nourishment. He's not letting her feed his soul. He's committing sacrilege."

Shaalon gasped. "Is that why he's done what he has, to use your resources?"

"Not entirely," Jakkon interjected. "He's afraid of our power. He knows what we can do."

"I see." Shaalon nodded. "It's wrong, what he's done. I do have the courage to stand with you all. I won't let Cayylen down."

Rexxon grinned. "Our wives will like you. You'll find your new sisters to be as loyal and likeminded as you are. We will take care of you. You are not alone."

She closed her eyes and let out a long sigh before she looked at them again. "Thank you. That's good to hear. I've worked in the palace kitchen to help support my family. My father was a soldier and as he aged his old injuries have caused him so much pain he can't serve anymore. I couldn't just stand by and watch that unfortunate woman die just because she wanted to save her husband, but I let my parents down. Now they have no one to take care of them. I can never go back."

Cayylen nodded. "A lot of people have been hurt, lost families, lost hope. We can't let the king continue to destroy everything good on Xerra. We need to restore the Mother to her rightful glory, and we need our lives back. We can't keep living in the shadows."

"Being forced to worship the Mother would be as bad as being unable to worship her," Shaalon said with passion. "Things need to change, but people need freedom, as well."

Rexxon frowned thoughtfully. "I agree with you. We do need to give people a choice. Faith shouldn't be dictated."

Out of the viewing window, Cayylen saw the moon base illuminated in the void of space. The sight was beautiful in a stark way. He held his woman's hand and prepared to do whatever it took to protect their future.

* * *

Shaalon stood in the center of the women, overwhelmed. There were ten couples here on the moon, the women all crowding around her. Many more families were on the surface in hiding. Those who had been caught or who stood up for the right to be together had been executed. Rexxon hadn't lied. The wives were very happy to meet her, and when she explained how she came to be Cayylen's a collective sigh left the crowd.

"That is the most romantic story I've ever heard," said Rexxon's wife, Alexa.

Alexa was very cute, and small compared to the people on Xerra. The woman appeared content in her polygamous marriage. This was surprising considering the part of Earth she claimed to hail from didn't allow these types of unions.

Crossing her arms over her chest, Shaalon pursed her lips. "How do we help in this war? What can we do up here when our husbands return to Xerra to fight?"

"I had no idea what I was getting into when I left Earth," Alexa said. "I just wanted to ensure my little sister's financial security. I've learned a lot about warriors and belonging to them. Our love, our bodies give them strength. We won't be staying here; we'll be going with them. They'll need our strength during the worst of the fighting."

"I can't fight." Shaalon frowned. "And please don't be offended, but you are very small compared to the king's youngest soldiers. How do you plan to go into battle?"

Alexa grinned. "You misunderstand me. My Xerraian isn't very good yet. We'll be staying in a protected encampment, and when our husbands need us, we'll be there to make love to them. They have a secret weapon the king wouldn't consider. Us."

She'd never thought of herself as a secret weapon before.

Tegan, Jakkon's wife, shrugged. She was also an earthling. "I've seen how wimpy those soldiers are compared to our warriors. They'll win. I'm just worried about the warriors working for us undercover and their families. My sister is on Xerra with her husband."

"Undercover?" Shaalon's brows rose.

"Yes. You'd be surprised how long they've planned this coup."

Shaalon's heart beat fast. Fear for Cayylen made her throat tight.

Alexa put her hand on Shaalon's shoulder. "It'll be okay. Our men are strong, and even stronger with us."

Tears welled in Shaalon's eyes, but she didn't let them fall.

"Go spend some time with Cayylen," Tegan suggested. "Such a new bond needs attention. Give him your love and make him strong for the battle ahead."

The human's wisdom couldn't be denied. She gave the women a small nod and left the group. Giggling trailed her as she walked down the narrow corridor from the common room to the hall where the bedroom she and Cayylen had been assigned stood. Shaalon approached the door and tapped lightly with her knuckle.

"Come in," Cayylen said.

Shaalon pushed open the door. "I thought you might need me."

Cayylen stood in the middle of the room. He was shirtless, and his pants hung low on his hips. His abs, the picture of male perfection, made her mouth go dry and the sexy "V" at his hips pointed to territory she wanted to explore again. The tight leather outlined an impressive bulge. In the dark cave, she hadn't had time to properly study his form.

Cayylen cleared his throat. "Eyes up here, wife."

Heat rushed into Shaalon's cheeks with blazing intensity. She met his beautiful dark eyes and saw his amusement, but also the hunger. A sexual charge filled the room. Shaalon licked her dry lips then cleared her throat. She'd come to offer herself to him, but now that she stood in the room shyness took over.

"I felt you coming to me. You want me as I want you. Let our bond flow through you. There is no reason for you to be afraid or embarrassed. I am your husband, and you are my wife. There's nothing about you that I don't long to see and touch. You are beautiful. I've been waiting for you." Cayylen grinned. "I need to be deep inside your hot, wet pussy."

Shaalon's cheeks burned hotter as arrows of need shot through her and desire flamed.

Cayylen took her in his arms. His spicy, masculine scent surrounded her as he led the way to the bed and laid her on the mattress. She looked up at him, uncertain what to do next. Her pussy ached. Something dark and primal lingered between them, and it made her forget she barely knew him. His gaze never left hers as he remained at the foot of the bed to remove his pants.

She bit her lip as she watched him. He was glorious. This connection between them was unlike anything she'd ever experienced. His lust fed hers, and she wanted him inside of her more than anything. She couldn't draw a full breath because the wanting hurt so much.

Her man had an amazing body, but every time her eyes wandered, the force of his gaze brought her attention back to his face. He crawled into bed next to her, shoving the thick fur blanket to the floor. She waited, completely dressed, but her husband was very naked next to her. She wanted to rip her clothing off. She couldn't breathe with him so close. He wasn't touching her, and she needed him to touch her.

"You have beautiful eyes." Cayylen pulled her close with a quick jerk. His lips brushed hers lightly, once, then twice. His hand slid up her back to cradle the back of her head, and he ran his fingers through the thickness of her long hair, pressing his mouth more firmly against hers. His shoulders were broad and muscular. She wrapped her arms around his neck, and the stubble on his jaw prickled against her face, but the sensation only added to Cayylen's raw male appeal. The strength of him took her breath away as her hands roamed his torso. She wanted to move lower, but a lingering shyness kept her hands away from his cock.

He deepened the kiss, sliding his tongue between her lips. She responded immediately, her tongue naturally following his lead. Prickles of desire awakened within her. Shaalon moaned against his lips as he tightened his arms around her.

He pulled away. Her eyes were still closed, but the heat of his mouth stayed close to hers. "I think you're overdressed."

"Being in your arms feels so right," she

whispered. "Please. I want to feel your skin against mine. I need you so much it hurts." Her pussy ached with wanting him.

She opened her eyes and watched him untie the wrap dress she wore. She'd donned a true bridal dress, in his family colors as well as her own. This traditional garment was a commitment and a promise. They were one for now and for always.

He put his hands under the sheer fabric and slowly inched it away from her breasts to expose her torso. Carefully, he pulled the material over her shoulders and off her arms until the dress came off.

Cayylen slipped his fingers into the waistband of her panties and grinned, pulling them off. She'd debated wearing the gifted Earth item, but now she was glad she'd listened to Alexa about the mystery of more clothing.

Sliding his hands down her legs in an erotic, albeit slow, seduction, he tormented her. When he finally reached her feet, he gently lifted her leg, running his fingers over her instep, before he put her foot down and repeated the process on the other foot. Shaalon watched him through a veil of lashes. She couldn't suppress her whimper of want. Her tongue darted out to wet her lower lip.

Cayylen smiled at her, his expression reverent. "By the Mother, you're beautiful. How did I ever deserve such a gift?" He straddled her on the bed and ran his hands over her flat stomach, then around her sides until he rubbed her lower back.

"You're blinded by lust," she teased.

"I know a beautiful body when I see it. I could come just looking at you."

Heat crept up her neck warming her cheeks. Shaalon bit her lip. "I want to touch you."

"I'd like that," he murmured.

She reached up and placed her palms flat on the center of his chest, feeling the hard muscles and the wiry sprigs of hair that covered his smooth skin. She brushed his nipples lightly, trailing her hand across his hard, ridged stomach. The man had amazing abs. She followed the thin trail of hair under his belly button. His groan made her bolder.

Shaalon grinned. "You are beautiful, too." Trailing her palms over his wide shoulders, she marveled at his strength. She ran her hands down his sides, stopping at his waist. He stiffened, and she grasped the base of his shaft, wrapping her hand tightly around him, and sliding down the length until her palm reached the head. Then she began exploring its width, feeling the channel and slit gently. He had a beautiful cock. Her other hand found his tight sac, fondling him until he moaned a soft masculine sound of pleasure.

Cayylen watched every movement with half closed eyes. She ran her hand lightly up and down his shaft and swirled the drop of moisture on the tip down the head. He shuddered under her touch.

"You're killing me, wife." Cayylen wrapped his arms around her, dragging her to him for another hard kiss and he pulled her on top of him as he lay down on the mattress. "I want to touch you -- taste you."

His gentle caress rolled over her skin. "Mmm, so soft." He kept caressing her, and the feathery strokes brought every inch of her skin to life. "Your softness is strength. In your arms, I am powerful."

"Do you mean that? Is it true that you will be able to fight harder because of our bond?"

"Yes, your love gives me a power unlike anything else. You are my salvation."

Shaalon kissed him softly, but then she became passionate as a fever for Cayylen raged in her soul. She wrapped her arms around his neck, clinging to him. Desire clouded her mind until she was high on him. His firm kiss intensified, and Shaalon closed her eyes relishing the sensation of his tongue darting between her lips. Drunk with desire for Cayylen, she groaned and ran her fingers through his hair. When she pulled back, his expression was unreadable.

"What are you thinking?"

"It's hard to think when you're looking at me with those beautiful eyes."

She closed them. "Is that better?"

"No. You're still distractingly beautiful." He sighed. "This battle that's coming is going to be unlike anything you've seen or experienced before."

Shaalon wanted to distract him from the darkness of his thoughts. She wasn't ready to face her fears for him yet. "Focus on winning. I have no fear because my soul is united to a husband who is the strongest warrior on Xerra. And his cock --" she reached down and stroked his length --"is rock hard."

"My temptress," he groaned. "You're the only woman I've ever wanted like this. You make me lose control." He nipped her earlobe. "I want you so bad it hurts."

She opened her eyes to bat her lashes at him, trying to look innocent. "*Me*?"

"You." Cayylen kissed her again, and she wrapped her arms around his neck. The mystical connection between them enriched the kiss until she wasn't sure if it was her lust or his making her desperate.

She lifted her hands, reaching up timidly to caress Cayylen's cheeks. His attention never left her face, and her hands shook as she ran her fingers down his neck and shoulders until she touched his defined six-pack abs. They kissed again with a breathless passion that sent joy coursing through her.

He pulled away and trailed his fingers over her nipple tweaking until she gasped. His hot gaze raked over her body and he cupped her breast running the pads of his callused thumbs over the sensitive nipples, eliciting a cry of enjoyment as he pinched the rosy nub gently. Desire curled in her belly as he drew her right nipple between his lips. He sucked hard, and she arched her back in response. His ministrations sent arrows of excitement through her. He moved to the left, and the cool air made the nipple damp from his attention tighten. She rubbed her legs together, needing his touch on her pussy, but he remained content to appreciate her breasts for the moment. Her arms wrapped around him and she stroked his neck and shoulders.

He kissed a trail down her stomach, and she shook with excitement as he moved closer to where she wanted him. Every inch of her skin became erogenous, and she relished his caresses. When he smiled, her heart twisted. He kissed the nest of hair on her mound, Shaalon whimpered. He was so close to giving her what she needed.

"Please," she managed to beg.

Cayylen chuckled. "What do you want Shaalon? Tell me. I want to hear you say the words."

* * *

"I want your mouth on me." Shaalon's cheeks were on fire, and she couldn't look him in the eyes.

"My mouth was on you. Tell me what you want."

"I want your mouth on my -- my pussy." Her

heart beat erratically.

"What do you want my mouth to do?"

"I want you to lick me," she whispered.

He pressed a long, reverent kiss against her mound. "I'm going to eat your pussy. I'm going to suck on your little clit just like those pretty nipples. I'm going to stick my fingers in your cunt until you scream. Tell me, and I'll do it. Say the words."

His voice was the sexiest thing she'd ever heard as he detailed what he wanted to do to her. She ached for him to fulfill his promise.

"Please," she begged.

"I'll please you if you just say the words, Cayylen said gazing at her with his beautiful dark eyes." I can feel your heart beating with my heart. You awe me, wife." His lips descended into a punishing kiss. When Cayylen pulled away, he bent to her breast and sucked hard on her nipple until he pulled away with a loud popping sound.

"I want to hear you beg for me," Cayylen said as he moved so quickly she had no time to think as he pinned her hands above her head. She lay trapped on the mattress, and her heart thundered in her ears. Cayylen gazed into her eyes as if she was the most amazing thing he'd ever seen. She could feel a heat creeping up her neck as he kissed her passionately until she erupted in flames. He let go of her arms and trailed his fingers over her breasts.

Shaalon's heart beat fast, and she had trouble drawing in a full breath. "I want you to suck on my clit, just like you did my nipples. I want your fingers inside me. Make me scream."

Shaalon arched her back, crying out. He slipped his hand between her legs, strumming her pleasure points. She whimpered.

He moved between her legs and separated her intimate folds and rubbed her clitoris. "Oh, sweetheart, you're so wet -- so perfect." He pressed his mouth against her clit, drawing the nub between his teeth as he sucked with the same force he'd used on her nipples, which made her back arch. She spread her legs wider and wiggled her hips.

He sucked and licked until she thrashed.

"Tell me you're mine." He pressed his mouth to her folds, sliding his tongue inside of her, fucking her with it before he pulled out and continued flicking her clit. He released her clit and lapped at the bud using long, lavishing strokes. Cayylen let go of her hands and slid his fingers inside of her, and she moaned. Two of his long digits found her g-spot. He drew hard on her clit, and she jerked.

"Cayylen! Oh yes!" Shaalon shook. "I'm so close!"

He made a sound deep in his throat as he worked her sensitive nub. She bucked uncontrollably under his mouth.

"Cayylen!" Shaalon saw sparks and her pussy clenched as she came -- hard. He continued the incredible assault on her clit.

Shaalon's fingers curled in Cayylen's hair, and she held him to her, screaming loud, primal cries of ecstasy. When she'd finished coming, he kissed her mound again.

He pushed loose tendrils of hair away from her face as he held her in his arms and gazed down at her adoringly. She sighed.

"I want to make you scream for me again while my cock is deep inside of you." Cayylen's sexy voice gave his words more seduction power.

"Get on your knees," he ordered, and she

scrambled to comply, spreading her legs wider, and he placed a kiss on her ass cheek as he slid his fingers into her tight pussy. She groaned.

"Tell me what you want Shaalon." He found her g-spot with his long index finger.

"I want you, Cayylen. Please."

"You want me to what?" His voice was a teasing seduction. "Tell me."

"Please, Cayylen," she begged. "I want your cock inside my pussy. I want it fast and hard."

He knelt behind her taking hold of her hips. The head of his cock touched her entrance as he slowly slipped inside of her. He stretched her; resistance gave way until his cock nestled sheathed from tip to base.

Every sensation pushed her closer to the edge. She bucked her hips under him. "Please, Cayylen." She begged. "I'm ready. I need you."

Cayylen's long fingers delved into her pussy while his thumb rolled against her clitoris. "Tell me you're mine." His husky voice made her shiver.

"I'm yours!" Shaalon panted. "I'm so close."

Cayylen straddled her on the bed.

"You were made for me," Cayylen said as he as he pressed his cock to her entrance and his girth and length filled her completely. She gasped. He pulled back and thrust forward. Cayylen adjusted his position, holding up her hips to angle deeper inside of her. His cock rubbed against her sweet spot with every stroke.

Cayylen moved faster with each stroke. He slammed into her with even more force than before. His cock brought a wave of pleasure so intense she bucked wildly. Their bodies collided in a sweaty dance. Each stroke angled just right, and the sensation caused her to release a sob of pure ecstasy. "Faster!"

His expression tightened with strain, but stroke after stroke he didn't come. Shaking and gasping from a release so intense it was almost painful she arched her back and wailed. Tears ran from the corners of her eyes. Her orgasm crested and crashed; she shattered against him. Pleasure shot through her, and she shook with gratification as he pumped. She saw sparks behind her eyelids as she shattered against him, whimpering as her bliss continued.

Cayylen held her hips and thrust faster until he threw back his head. "Shaalon!" Her name reverberated through the room with primal energy. Giving a harsh masculine grunt, he stiffened, thrust a final time and the heat of his release filled her.

"I love you," Shaalon gasped out as she watched him come.

Cayylen pulled out from between her legs as he collapsed beside her and held her close. He buried his face in the hair curling in the crook of her neck, kissing her there as the embers of passion cooled.

"You're amazing." He pressed his lips to hers, and she closed her eyes. He deepened the kiss, but then pulled away to look at her. For a moment, they said nothing.

"We will win this war," Cayylen promised. "I swear to you, we will win. Our children will inherit Xerra, and we will have peace and prosperity.

Shaalon snuggled down deeper into the warmth of his arms. "I hope you're right."

"I am," he said smugly. "With you in my bed, I'll be as strong as an army all on my own. With so many of us in Soul Unity and Soul Trinity, we're ten times as strong as the king's military."

"Don't tell me falsehoods to steal my fears. I can be brave for you, even if the truth isn't pretty."

Cayylen chuckled. "I wouldn't lie to you. Not when you're carrying my child."

Gasping, Shaalon sat up. "So soon? How can you be so sure?"

He cupped her cheek and stroked her face with his thumb. The tenderness in his expression made her heart ache. "Our bond told me the moment my seed took root." He touched her abdomen reverently. "This. This is our future. You've given me the greatest gift. Thank you, wife. You are the most incredible blessing the Mother has ever given me. Even if I had to take on the king's army single handed I would win because I'm fighting for you and our baby. I love you, Shaalon."

"And I love you. Whatever the future holds, I will stand by your side."

She put her head down on his chest and listened to his heart beating. This was the calm before the storm, but Shaalon wasn't afraid of the coming tempest because Cayylen's love was the strongest shelter she'd ever known. They would win the war. Of that she had no doubt.

Kiijan (Married to the Aliens 4)
Ashlynn Monroe

Kiijan's parents were the foundation of the revolution to bring back the ways of the warriors. She's lived her life under the shadow of their names. She longs to travel to Earth, her mother Alexa's homeland, and be who she is, not the daughter of revered heroes or the wife of a warrior. However, the best-laid plans sometimes go awry.

Rieggar has always planned to take a demure wife. His life has been dedicated to training and spiritual education. He's never considered love as essential in drawing the power of a woman into himself -- until he meets a stowaway.

Kiijan knows her only way to Earth is to run away, but when she meets the captain of *Revolution*, the ship she picked to escape on, he gives her two choices. She can go to the airlock or his bed. She is enough of her mother's daughter to choose to die in the vacuum of space rather than surrender, but the passion in Rieggar's gaze tempts her to fight a battle she's not sure she'll win. Can she seduce this warrior into giving her the freedom she's always craved?

Chapter One

"No, father," Kiijan said in a steady, albeit firm tone. Inside she was terrified, but she kept the fear from showing. Turning to her other father, she scowled. "Please don't tell me you've actually reached an agreement."

Her mother cleared her throat. "We have." Alexa spoke before either of Kiijan's fathers could. "We just want what's best for you."

"Best for *me*? Or best for your legacy?" Kiijan was the youngest and the only daughter. They needed her to marry a warrior or two, but she had no desire to follow in their footsteps. "I'm my own woman. I want to be free."

Rexxon, her heart father, stood up so fast his chair fell, clattering to the floor, as he glowered down at Kiijan. "Daughter, have you ever seen us mistreat or even try to control your mother?"

She shrugged. "I've also never seen you let her travel without one of you. She doesn't have her own money. She can't do anything without your permission. I want to build a life as my brothers have, not be given away from one set of rule-makers to another."

Rexxon turned to Tavvor, Kiijan's biological father. "I told you it was a bad idea for her to travel to Earth and stay with her aunt."

Tavvor glared. "I wasn't pleased she visited. If you recall, our wife was the one who insisted. She --"

"See?" Kiijan interrupted. "You see women as property, not people. You had no problem at all when any of my brothers traveled off world. Jallen is on Earth right now, and I haven't heard either of you grumble about his trip."

"Jallen is looking for a wife. He wanted a human woman, even though he'd have his pick of Xerrian brides." Tavvor cleared his throat and looked away. "But I will not see my daughter marry a weak human male."

"All six of your sons are half human, as am I."

"That's different. You also have our blood. Jallen is strong and can protect his human, but you need a warrior, not -- as your mother would say -- a wuss."

Kiijan crossed her arms over her chest. "Not every man has to fight to prove his strength."

Tavvor's eyebrows rose. "He does if he wants to marry our daughter."

"Ahh!" Kiijan shook her fists in front of her. "You don't own me." She turned to Rexxon. "Either of you."

Rexxon nodded. "Of course we don't, but we love you. We have seen lesser men fall to our swords. Our faith has given us youth beyond what other men enjoy. Your mother doesn't look any older than the day we married her because she *chose* us." He sighed and rubbed the bridge of his nose. "I just don't want you to regret your mate -- mates. Two loving warriors will protect you and see that you and your children want for nothing. How could we wish anything else for you?"

"Dad." Kiijan turned from Rexxon to address Tavvor. "Dads. I want a different kind of marriage. I want to be an equal partner, not a prisoner."

Tavvor chuckled. "No man would be foolish enough to harm our daughter."

Kiijan huffed out with disgust. "That's part of the problem. I don't want to be anyone's daughter or wife. I want to be *me*. I don't want my spouse to treat me a certain way based on fear or some obsession with my family."

"I think you're overreacting." Rexxon's even tone belied the anger that flashed in his eyes. "You fear nothing."

"I fear everything," she countered. "Just because you don't see the truth doesn't mean I'm wrong."

Tavvor frowned. "It is done. You will wed the warrior we've deemed worthy. You've always known we would pick your first husband. Even your mother agreed with our decision. We've seen to your future safety. This argument is pointless. I'm sure he'll bring a second husband, but at this time you'll marry Xieen and only Xieen."

Kiijan stopped her tapping toe and forced her stance to relax. Taking a deep breath, she let it out slowly, and willed her fathers to understand. "You're wrong."

"We are not. Give Xieen a chance. He is smart, strong, and loyal. What more could you want in your mate?"

She grimaced. "How about love?"

Tavvor put his hand on her shoulder. "Do you believe your mother loves us?"

"Of course. She adores you both."

"She didn't even know us on our wedding day. We picked her, she didn't pick us."

"That doesn't mean I'll be happy with the same kind of marriage. I want to go back to Earth. Aunt Sofia said she'd be happy to have me stay with her. She's so much fun! I love hearing stories about what Mom was like as a teenager."

"Your aunt isn't Xerrian." Tavvor crossed his arms over his chest. "She'll never understand what it is to be a part of our world. She's not one of us."

Kiijan felt heat rush into her cheeks, and she

fought the urge to cry. She didn't want her fathers to see her as childish or weak. They were in a battle -- a battle she intended to win. "Do you consider me lesser because my mother is human?"

Rexxon scowled. "You know we would never feel that way about you. Daughter, be reasonable."

"I want a life that I choose. I want to live on Earth."

Both of her fathers gapped at her. "Out of the question!" they shouted in perfect synchronicity.

Kiijan flinched. "Do you even care what I want?"

"You will marry. It has been decided," Rexxon said.

Tavvor nodded. "There is no further discussion. You will stay here, with your family, where you are safe."

"Aunt Sofia is family too!" Her throat tightened.

Rexxon's face grew fierce. His battle-scarred visage was far from beautiful, but his eyes were always kind, until now. He'd never looked at her like that before, and his anger cracked her heart so deeply she felt a physical ache in her chest. "Father... "

"You will marry!"

She turned from them, the two most important men in her world, and wiped at the angry tears she couldn't hold back any longer. Letting go of a shaky breath, she straightened her shoulders and, without looking back, walked out of the room.

* * *

Rieggar missed the days of battle, but the great war was over, and they'd won. Shipping Xerrian art to Earth had proven lucrative, though not without risk. A run of bad luck had drained his accounts. He rubbed the ache from an old wound that had never healed right. He'd been one of the first to become a warrior during the revolution, but even with the healing power of his adopted religion, he wasn't a young man.

Maybe if he'd taken a woman things would have been different for him, but his mind was broken from the horrors he'd witnessed. When he'd made the choice to leave his brotherhood after the war he'd angered many of his comrades who'd fought hard to restore the rule of warriors. He'd decided to live the life of a civilian, but deep down he was still a warrior. He still went to the temple to worship and drink the healing Mother's Milk, but he had no interest in politics. He refused to dictate the lives other men led.

Gazing out the starboard window of his beloved ship the *Revolution* he contemplated the vast velvet darkness of space. The stars were beautiful. They reminded him of why he picked this life. Freedom.

He pushed away his dark mood. Without normal sun cycles, the sameness left him with a melancholy he couldn't shake. He rubbed his old injury harder, sighing. "I'm happy with my life," he muttered, unsure why he felt the need to say the words aloud.

"Captain!" shouted Ellar, the *Revolution*'s first officer. "You need to come to the cargo hold."

"What's the emergency?" Rieggar pressed his fingers to his temples. "Can this wait?"

"You'll want to see."

Intrigued, Rieggar turned from his view of the stars. He stared down his most trusted ally, one of his dark eyebrows quirked up. "Will I?"

"You will." Ellar nodded. "Believe me, you will."

"Go on?"

"I want to see the look on your face. Come see my surprise."

Rieggar rubbed his temples. "I don't enjoy games, and I'm not in the mood for joviality."

"Our guest is a complication, not a game."

"Guest?" Rieggar scowled. "We have a stowaway?"

"Come see for yourself." Ellar chuckled. "You're never going to believe who she is. As angry as I am about what this means to our journey, I'm going to enjoy telling this story when we return home."

"She?" Rieggar scowled. He couldn't care less who she was. A delay would cost him, and he needed this trip to be profitable. "Just tell me."

Ellar's smile slid off his face. "I'm sorry. I know how vital this delivery is."

"Well? Who is our unwanted passenger?" Glowering, he walked over to the captain's seat, sat, and checked the navigation. After making several adjustments, he stood up and turned toward his business partner. "Is returning to the planet our only option, or can we just keep the female onboard?"

"I think we should return to Xerra. The daughter of Tavvor and Rexxon is sleeping in our hold. Her fathers won't be pleased."

Rieggar's eyes widened. The warriors were legendary, and the fact their youngest child, and only daughter, was beloved to them was common knowledge. She was a desirable mate, and he'd heard the fathers had been turning away interested males for years. "What is she doing here?"

Ellar grimaced. "Do not look at me as if this is my doing. I just found her. Let's wake her, and she can regale us with the story on our way home."

Resentment crept through Rieggar. "Or she can tell us quickly before I toss her out the airlock. Why would she pick our shipment for her stunt?"

"I wish I knew, but she's here. There's not much we can do now, so we might as well just accept the loss. I'll bill the fathers a standard fee. That will help recover some of our loss. I'm sure they can afford it. I have no doubts Yeelee will steal this buyer from us."

"I hate losing anything to that underhanded bastard!"

"As do I." Ellar sighed. "But there's nothing to be done. If she's tracked here and we don't bring her home, the consequences to our business will end us."

Rieggar nodded. As usual, his level-headed associate was right, but that didn't make him happy about what they had to do.

* * *

Kiijan woke with a start. She had no idea where she was. Disorientation left her terrified for a moment. Memories of sneaking onboard the ship headed to Earth came flooding back. She shivered. She'd made sure this model ship had a heated hold before making her final choice, but she had no idea that they were going to be so stingy with that feature. The manifest had only said "art". She should have picked a ship carrying something that required a warmer temperature. Her neck ached from sleeping in the awkward space.

Noise. She stilled. They weren't far enough from home. She couldn't be discovered. Something touched her arm. She flinched and rolled to her side. In the dim emergency lighting, she saw the silhouette of a male staring into her hiding place.

The hold lit up brightly, and she blinked as her eyes adjusted to the sudden change. "Pleasant waking," said the most handsome man she'd ever seen. "Now tell me why the hell you're on my ship."

Well, Hottie hadn't wasted any time letting her know she was unwelcome.

Her whole body tensed. Trembling, Kiijan forced

her face to remain impassive. Her natural response to being caught was to cower, but she resisted. Showing fear was not the way of the warrior, and she came from a long line of fighters.

The man staring down at her grinned as if he could read her mind, and she narrowed her eyes at him. His dark brown eyes twinkled, amused, and his kissable lips remained quirked in a half smile. He was as massive as he was attractive. His goatee matched the dark locks left long and unrestrained around his rugged face. A scar by his temple only added to his good looks.

The trace of stubble along his jaw line begged for her touch, but she managed to keep her hands to herself. He was tan, too tan for a man in his sunless line of work. His dark hair bore traces of the sun's kiss, too, as streaks of light brown mingled with the darker locks in a way that was too natural to be a style choice. Something about this pilot didn't add up. He reminded her of one of her father's warriors. He was just too much man to be average.

He must be the captain, Rieggar -- the ex-warrior who'd caused such a stir after the war when he renounced his position of leadership in the government.

He offered her his hand. "Come with me."

Kiijan wanted to refuse. For the first time in her life, there wasn't anyone who would protect her, and the realization made her feel a keen sense of more loss than fear. Guilt ate into her soul. If she was never found, her fathers and mother would die mourning her. "Why?"

"Because you are not cargo. Come. It has been a full day cycle since take off, you must be hungry."

He was right. She'd packed survival rations but

had decided to nibble on them sparingly. She could survive on what she had, but real food was much more tempting. "I'm fine."

His eyes narrowed. "Lying about your hunger serves no purpose. I will not poison you. I'm much more likely to jettison you for stowing away than waste good poison on you."

Her eyes widened. "I will pay you double the normal fee for transport to Earth. My death would be painful for my family. I pray you reconsider."

A look of something akin to regret passed over his features. "By the Mother, I would not murder a woman, no matter how complicated she just made my life. Come. I jest with you. I won't jettison you, at least not until you've had an ample final meal."

He had a terrible sense of humor. Pursing her lips, she took a moment before nodding. "Thank you." She accepted his hand and wiggled out of her tight nook. Her knees popped as she stood, and she stretched.

"You're taller than I thought you'd be," he said seriously. Then he grinned. "Follow me."

She trailed behind him out of the crowded hold into a very modern hall. His ship was older, but clearly well cared for. The traces of in-progress cosmetic work made her consider her "host" in a new perspective. More guilt hit her. This was his home and his livelihood. She was an unexpected interloper. "I'm sorry. I am serious about paying you for transporting me to Earth. Warriors fought for freedom, but that didn't seem to extend to their wives and daughters," she apologized softly. "My name is Kiijan."

He grunted, nodded, but didn't look at her. "I know who you are. What motivates your desperation? A lover waiting on Earth, or something else?"

"Typical male." Kiijan shook her head, frowning. "My fathers have decided they'd like me to marry. They've decided who I should marry. I want the same choices as my brothers have. I am going to live with my aunt."

"So, you disagree with The Mother's wisdom that men should protect the women they love?"

"I disagree with a great many things, but never that. However, most males do not understand what The Mother means. My own fathers are confused right now."

He paused. She couldn't help grinning at how scandalized he appeared. She started walking forward toward the bridge. Moments later, he followed her.

"Do you know the ship's layout?" he asked with just a hint of condescension.

She glanced up at him. "I researched many things about this ship, including you and your manifest, before taking the risk of stowing away."

This time his surprise morphed into curiosity. "And?"

"And I thought you were my best chance. Your flight log is very impressive, and yes, I know how to read a flight log."

"I fought with your fathers in the war."

Her shoulders sagged. "I assumed."

"I have to return you."

"No, you don't. I promise I won't be a burden to you. I can pay generously, and I will, as soon as we reach Earth, but I won't go back. They have no way of knowing I'm here. Give me my freedom."

He reached out and gently stopped her before a door. "Open." The portal swished softly to allow them entry. She followed him into the room. Quality radiated from everything in the small cabin. "This is our best cabin. You will remain here until I have decided what to do about your *request*. I once felt as if I'd never be free, so I do know what you're going through, but I have obligations, and this decision affects more than just me." He spun on his heel and left so fast she didn't have a chance at a rebuttal.

Rushing forward she pressed the door pad, but it didn't open. "Damn it." She leaned her head against the cool metal, and closed her eyes. "Mother, if you're listening, help me. We both know I'm not built to be the kind of wife a warrior wants. Give me my freedom."

Chapter Two

"Give me my freedom." The words radiated through Rieggar. He couldn't un-hear her words. The plea in her crystalline blue eyes had torn into his resolve. She was beautiful. Blonde hair was rare on Xerra, and hers begged for his touch. For her to risk her life to leave the planet she had to be truly desperate. Alone in space, he could have his way with her and toss her out the airlock, and no one would be the wiser.

She wanted the same thing he'd spent his whole life pursuing. Choice. He'd fought hard for his, and now he held hers in his hands. When he got to the bridge, he paused at the sound of Ellar shouting.

"We will have your money," Ellar insisted.

"If you are unable to pay the full amount I will reclaim the ship. You shouldn't have risked her if you didn't believe you could pay me on time." The tone the creditor used was completely remorseless. The man had scammed them, but when the *Revolution* had been dead in the sky, they'd ignored reason and accepted the lender's offer. Now two shipment issues had put them behind schedule on repayment, and the situation was dire.

Ellar cleared his throat. "Understood." The buzz of an empty channel indicated the creditor had terminated the signal. "May your entrails be boiled and eaten!"

Rieggar entered. The bridge needed a lot of work. She was an old ship, but she was theirs -- for now. "He refused to grant an extension?"

"Of course. He wants our ship. May the bastard's cock rot from his body. If we take the woman back we'll lose everything, but we have no choice."

Rieggar pushed his hair out of his eyes and sat

down at the helm. If he turned the ship around, they all lost. If he went to Earth and the fathers traced her escape to them, they'd never get another shipping contract, and they'd be ruined. His fingers hovered over the touchscreen. And then inspiration struck.

"Our guest is wealthy. Her bridal money would take care of our problem. Her fathers would never destroy her husband and risk hurting her." His fingers flew over the log. "I've just made you acting captain. If my negotiation goes as planned, you'll be performing a wedding."

"Rieggar, don't do this. Things are already bad."

"Trust me."

Ellar sighed. "My friend, I hate it when you say that, but I will. Don't make me regret it."

"Keep us on course for Earth."

Ellar paled. "I hope you know what you're doing."

"Do I ever?"

Ellar didn't appear amused as Rieggar stood and left the bridge.

* * *

Rieggar knocked on the door. He didn't need to, the ship was his to command, but the woman certainly was not-yet.

"Enter." The door opened, and he entered carrying the tray of food. He set the burden down on the table and began setting two places. "I hope you don't mind that I eat with you. I would like to extend an offer to you." This would be so much easier on him if she wasn't so beautiful.

"Offer?" One of her delicate blonde brows rose. Her nose wrinkled in a way that made her pixie-like face even more beautiful.

He straightened his back and reminded himself

this was a business deal. "I have been a poor host. We both have something the other values. Forgive me for neglecting a respectful introduction when we met earlier. I am Rieggar. Just Rieggar. I am not a part of the elite class. I gave up my status. You need freedom and I need money. We have the power to give each other something. There is no way for me to just deposit you on Earth without your fathers destroying me financially, you know that."

She looked away. He was right. Shame filled her. "What do we do?"

"We marry,   in Earth airspace, in an Earth ceremony. I will give you the kind of marriage you'd have with an Earth man. In turn, you will pay off the debt over my ship. You will be welcome to live with me on this ship, or you may remain on Earth."

He waited. She blinked at him, and her brows drew together. Then she stood and went to sit at the table. She began to fill the plate in front of her.

He wasn't sure what game she played, but he took his cue from her actions and sat down. He watched her for a long moment while she ignored him completely and then he put some of the food on his own plate. Even though they had a superior food generator, the first bite tasted like nothing because his mouth was so dry. She didn't appear nervous at all. She ate as if he hadn't just made a life-changing proposal.

Rieggar could stand the suspense no longer. "Well?" He hadn't meant to sound so gruff.

She glanced up. "The protein is excellent. Thank you."

He scowled. "You can't ignore away my request for a union."

"I thought I was doing an admirable job of

trying. I can't believe you're serious about this."

"I am. I swear to you that I will not control you. In Earth airspace, a marriage performed by a ship's captain is recognized as legitimate. We'll even use Earth vows and radio a registration before performing the ceremony. The radio room controllers can act as witnesses. We will need to consummate the union, but I promise to be considerate. This protects you from your fathers rushing to Earth to reclaim you, and it saves my ship. I can't think of a better solution."

She took another bite, chewed thoughtfully, and put down her fork. "When I said that most males misinterpret The Mother I was serious. Tell me what you think protecting your wife means."

The bite he tried to swallow stuck in his throat. He managed to ingest the nutrient with as much dignity as he could manage under the circumstances. "Why are you playing with me, woman?"

"I never play. This is war, and I want to know my opponent better."

"Ah. The old Earth adage about love and war?"

Sadness passed through her eyes. "I've always known marriage would never be about love, but if I can at least ensure happiness, I'll be satisfied with your proposal."

He stalled by taking another bite. Milling over her words, he realized she was a warrior and he needed to answer her in that respect. "The Mother is wise, but sadly mortals are not. If you consent to be my wife, I will not stop you from living as you choose, even if I would not choose the path for you. If I follow you down a road, I will walk beside you, not ahead of you. I will not let my need to see to your physical well-being impede your mental well-being."

She sat back and studied his face. He took

another bite. She was right. He'd seen men force feed their mate and bind them against their will in the name of protection. He'd heard of women who even feared their mates, which given the natures of the warrior's bond with a true mate, he couldn't fathom. Marrying her would destroy his chance at ever knowing what it felt like to have a true mate, but at least his life would never be dull -- providing she didn't stay on Earth.

Kiijan wiped moisture from her eyes with the back of her hand. "I'm sorry. This is a hard decision for both of us. Circumstance has put us in a place where there is no easy choice. Thank you for giving me more of an option than just returning to my family in disgrace to live a life under constant surveillance." She took a shaky breath. "I agree to your terms. I should compose a message to my family. We need to do this before my aunt is notified of my arrival because she'll see right through the farce and try to intercede."

Her use of *farce* hurt, but he wasn't sure why. The sadness in her expression distressed him. "I will not hurt you. I would welcome you to live on this ship and travel with me. If you decide to stay on Earth, I understand, but for the sake of appearances consider making a few trips with me before staying on Earth permanently."

"You are admirably sensible." She nodded. "I would love a visit, at least a day, with my aunt, but I would be honored to fly with you once or twice."

Her words hit him in the pit of his stomach. There was no reason for him to take offense, but he did. Rieggar stood. "I'll send Ellar for the tray. We travel with a limited crew for financial reasons, but since that will change when we return, this will be the only journey where you'll have to make do with our clumsy efforts."

"If I am free to move about the ship as I please, I can take care of these dishes myself. I am competent."

She surprised him again, but he nodded. "I have very little to offer you, but consider this your home."

Her soft smile warmed him for no reason. "Thank you," Kiijan said. "I will do what I can not to be a burden." She raised her glass. "To a mutually beneficial partnership."

Ironically, he'd made the same toast when Ellar had joined him in business. He nodded brusquely and began leaving, trying not to let her see how he was torn between relief and irritation.

A thought gave him pause and just before he left the room he turned back to her. "Are you in love with another man?"

"Would that change anything?"

His heart sank. The idea of her being in love bothered him more than it should. "No. Forgive me for asking." He left the room.

* * *

"She's in love with another man," Rieggar said.

"Who?"

"I don't know, but I'm sure she has a lover."

Ellar scowled. "Will he be a problem?"

"I doubt it. If he was able to marry her, he'd have done so."

"Good." Ellar smiled. "Now lighten up, my friend, we're entering Earth's airspace. I'll get your bride. Radio in and let them know we need some witnesses for the wedding. It's been a long time since anyone from Xerra had a wedding in the space over Earth. The war ended the need for that, so the novelty should ensure they honor our request."

Ellar hurried out, happy, excited. Rieggar wished he could find joy in this too, but the beautiful woman he was marrying wasn't really going to be his. It shouldn't bother him, but it did. Women flocked to him in every port. He could have married countless women, but now they were just a faceless blur. He'd never wanted a woman that didn't want him -- until now. To his horror, he realized he was infatuated with his bride and losing control over the situation -- fast.

* * *

Kiijan hadn't taken anything but nourishment with her when she'd fled. She'd never imagined she'd be getting married in clothing she'd worn for days, and to a man she barely knew. He wanted her money, and she wanted his promise of control over her own life. She'd dreamed of at least marrying a man who thought she was beautiful. She hadn't told Rieggar she found him attractive. Following Ellar, a pleasant man with a great sense of humor, to her doom -- wedding ceremony -- she tried not to think about how much she was looking forward to consummating her marriage. At least they were doing everything in the traditional Earth style, with no witness to the consummation.

She knew the dynamics, had shared a few stolen kisses in her youth, but she'd saved herself for this man. Knowing he didn't care made waiting feel ridiculous, but she hoped he'd respect her for giving him the honor, if nothing else.

When the door to the bridge opened with its familiar swish, her breath caught and heat filled her cheeks. Rieggar stood on the bridge looking surreal. He'd put on some of the finest ceremonial clothing she'd ever seen. The effort he'd made with his appearance honored her. Her heart beat faster when he smiled at her. If she were a fool, she'd fall in love with this man.

She moved to him, ignoring the interested parties

watching from the open comm link. Her eyes remained fixed on her groom. He held out his hand, and she took it. He shook. She glanced down at their joined hands and then up to his face again. He smiled at her with an expression she couldn't define. Before she could focus too much on it, Ellar cleared his throat. He began in English to befit the Earth witnesses. Her gaze found Rieggar's, and she responded to Ellar's questions in a disembodied way as she let his dark eyes consume her. His fingers tightened around hers. His body would unite with hers, very soon. Her breath hitched.

"By the authority of my commission as captain and under the laws governing the space surrounding the planet Earth, I now pronounce you man and wife. You may kiss the bride," Ellar said.

The Earthlings clapped. She ignored everything as Rieggar's arms came around her. He pressed his mouth to hers. The gentle pressure exploded into an urgent demand she returned with equal need.

When Rieggar pulled away, he was panting and flushed. He cupped her cheek. "My wife," he said simply. Then without a word he picked her up and strode out of the room without a backward glance. The hooting from their video guests died as the door shut behind them. He held her close as he carried her past her room. "I want to do this in my room, all right?"

She didn't know what to say. His every action was far more possessive than she'd expected. Having him welcome her to his personal space made her feel cherished in a way she couldn't define. She nodded. He kissed her forehead. "I promise this will be good." His eyes darkened, and his brows drew together. "Let me know what you need."

She didn't know how to tell him she had no idea.

The door to his room opened for them, and she

was greeted by his scent that was a combination of male and a spicy musk that sent her pulse racing. The room was tidy, and the bed made. There were few personal artifacts around the room, but she did see the curved sword he'd surely carried in battle hanging on one wall.

He set her on her feet and gathered the hair that flowed around her shoulders so he could lift it away from her neck. She stood motionless as he kissed her under her ear before nuzzling her neck, breathing her in loudly. She shivered.

"I want you, woman," he whispered in her ear.

"I -- I'm not on any kind of birth prevention," she whispered back, trying to get the practical business out of the way.

"I have nothing here for prevention. I am fond of children, but never gave them much consideration. If my seed grows in you, I will do my best to be worthy of that honor. I am willing to take the chance."

She bit her lip. Surprisingly, she was too. She brushed his overly long hair out of his eyes. He leaned down and claimed her lips again. Desire flamed to life inside of her. She might not have experience, but she wasn't afraid to show this man she could possess him as easily as he'd carried her away from their wedding.

Finding her courage, Kiijan approached making love like the warrior she was at heart. She closed her eyes, exhaled, and focused on slowing her racing heart as she attacked first in this war of passion. Her gaze found his, and she began disrobing. Methodically, she removed everything until she stood naked. As he watched her, she noticed the outline of his cock bulge against the leather of his pants.

"You're overdressed, husband." Kiijan reached for him.

Chapter Three

Rieggar's abs tightened as Kiijan ran her fingers over his waistband. He made a slight grunting sound but didn't move as Kiijan worked the leather down over his hips, further down his thighs, and then off. Rieggar let out a long, slow breath and she ran her hands down his lower back, the hard muscles of his ass, and the backs of his thighs. He widened his stance, and his erection bobbed. He'd never been so aroused in his life.

"You are a bold surprise." He'd expected a virgin bride, and the flare of jealousy he felt as he decided she wasn't shocked him. He was glad she wasn't frigid or terrified, but the idea some other male had touched his woman made his nostrils flare and fists clench. His anger evaporated as she ran her soft fingers over him.

Kiijan got down on her knees in front of Rieggar. Her beautiful blue eyes made his breath catch expectantly when she glanced up at him. This woman was his. His heart beat painfully. The Mother had given him an amazing gift. Now all he had to do was figure out a way to keep her.

She appeared to enjoy the curves and planes of his body as she ran her hands over him. He wanted her to touch his cock, but she didn't. She traced the masculine "V" at his hips and brushed his skin gently, but always her touch moved away seconds before she caressed his genitals.

Kiijan kissed him where the hair trailed just under his belly button. He groaned. She blew a gentle stream of air along his shaft and leaned forward to follow the air with her tongue. She lapped at him slowly until he shivered. When she glanced up, their gazes locked. Electricity sizzled between them. She drew him deeply into her mouth. Her eyes closed and her small mouth explored every ridge and vein. Her blissful expression only made him hotter, and he couldn't stop watching her.

His ass clenched, and his knees jerked with the effort to remain standing as pleasure coursed through him. He held the base of her skull gently as he closed his eyes to relish what she did to him.

"Princess, my sweet princess," he breathed. The endearment fit, and he knew from that moment on he'd slay every dragon that threatened her and do everything he could to become her castle. She wanted freedom, but he wanted her.

She lavished his length with attention, but when she turned those long slow licks on his sac, his knees did buckle. He had to hold the wall for support. She ran her nails gently over his lower back and ass. He shivered and cried out. His balls were painfully tight.

Rieggar was so close, but he refused to let her rob him of the joy of her pussy. He pulled her to her feet. Her eyes widened for a second before he crushed his lips to hers. He wasn't tender as he held her in his arms. A possessive need he'd never experienced with any other woman roared to life. She was limp in his arms for a second before her arms tightened around his neck. When she kissed him back, he groaned and held her tighter.

He slid his hands under her ass and picked her lithe body up. She wrapped her legs around his hips. He felt her wetness against his shaft. He'd never been with a woman who was so responsive. Her sexuality pleased him. The fact that his body had made her so ready wasn't lost on him. She was amazing. He'd erase the memory of any other man's touch. The kiss never broke as he moved to the bed, still holding her tight.

He wanted to ask if her lover had kissed her this intimately and decided against risking the moment. Perhaps her lover was not worthy of her or inexperienced in how to please a woman. He'd show her he was more than capable of giving her pleasure.

* * *

Kiijan was in control until Rieggar lifted her off the floor. His powerful strength displayed as his mouth continued to press against hers, his hot mouth feeding her lust, nourishing her soul. His muscles flexed, tensing, as he carried her to his bed.

She gazed up at him as the kiss broke and he hovered over her. He touched her face, and his gaze seemed to be searching her expression. "For this moment, you're mine."

She should be horrified. Those words were everything she feared. Yet instead of terror, he inspired lust to bloom inside of her. Rieggar eased her thighs apart, opening her to him. He lavished attention on her clit. She jerked at his touch, shocked. It was easy to be bold when she was caressing him, but no one had made her feel like this before.

Rieggar lapped at her pussy as if he'd never tasted anything so sweet. At first, she was quiet, and then her whimpers grew. He lapped faster, harder. She tangled her fingers in his hair, bucking against his face. Kiijan cried out, and he didn't stop. She was breathing harder, and her whimpers grew more desperate. She moved toward the precipice of something wonderful. She'd heard this moment described by other women, but they hadn't done it justice. She squeezed her eyes tighter, and a keening escaped her in a wail. Kiijan came for him, but he didn't let up.

"Rieggar!" she cried. "More!" Then she moaned a long, unintelligible sound. Her hips jerked off the bed as she squealed with pleasure.

He replaced his tongue with a large finger but paused.

"You're a virgin?" He appeared shocked.

"Of course. Why would you doubt that?"

He flushed. "Because I'm a fool. Forgive me, princess. I'm not worthy of you." He kissed her again, and the frown creasing her brow relaxed. She kissed him back.

When he pulled away, she groaned with disappointment, but he used his tongue to build her need back into an inferno again. He continued until she cried out again, coming ferociously. He cupped her breasts tenderly, flicking her nipples with his thumbs as he watched her. His intense gaze made her feel both safe and exposed in the same moment. She couldn't pull away from the gravity in his expression, and he held her entranced as pleasure tingled through her.

He smiled. "Beautiful."

His soft voice broke the spell, and Kiijan closed her eyes and wailed her pleasure. She gasped, jerking as he put his mouth on her left breast. His lips were warm and wet. She shivered as Rieggar drew hard on the sensitive peak. Pleasure burned hotter in her core. "Yes," she panted. "Yes!" Her breath grew uneven, and she saw sparks behind her eyelids as she shattered, hard, against his hand while mewing little whimpers. Her raging flames cooled to embers, and her pussy contracted with the echoes of her orgasm as she lay in the blissful place Xerrians called The Between, a space where her soul wasn't fully connected to her body, and she felt like she was floating. Relaxation flowed through her. She ignored the warning, nagging her consciousness, that a bond could form between them.

When she came back from the floating depths of

ecstasy, she looked to see Rieggar kneeling between her legs. He dropped a kiss on her thigh. Kiijan gasped and gazed down at her warrior helplessly. Her pussy contracted with the echoes of her orgasm. Sexual education for Xerrians was very thorough, so even though she was a virgin she knew they weren't done, and she wanted more.

His lust, almost palpable around them like a great unseen entity, seemed to radiate into her. Kiijan's want escalated with the desire in his expression. His passion made her hot. Her breath caught the moment his gaze captured hers. He trapped her on the mattress by placing his large hands on either side of her as he hovered over her. Her breathing grew shallow, and Rieggar groaned.

He rolled beside her, propping himself up with one arm so he could put his free hand between her legs. The sensation caused her to buck her hips and grind her clit against his touch. He chuckled. "Do you like that, my sweet stowaway?"

She bit her lip and nodded fast. Her eyes fluttered closed, and a soft sound of pleasure escaped her.

He kissed her quickly and pulled back. "Amazing." He rubbed her clit while his index finger delved inside to caress her G-spot. Kiijan whimpered as her desire sparked into flames. She pressed against him.

"What do you want, little stowaway?"

Her eyes opened. Their gazes locked. "More. Faster." Her vision hazed with lust.

He made a sound -- something between a moan and a growl. "Always look at me when you beg for what you want. You have beautiful eyes."

Kiijan's face heated. She didn't look away.

Prickles of awareness stirred in her womb, and her pussy responded. Her small fingers trailed lightly down his stubbled jaw. She put her hands on the back of his neck and pulled him to her lips. He choked out an emotional grunt and kissed her back with a ferocity that stole her thoughts. She lost her soul in him.

Rieggar sat up, taking her with him, and pulling her to sit on his lap, facing him. She rubbed her wetness against the warrior's thigh. His erection pressed against her hip, proof of his desire. He cradled the right side of her face in his large, warm hand and she turned into his palm, placing a tender kiss there.

"I can feel your heart beating with my heart," Rieggar whispered. "You awe me, woman."

She snuggled her cheek into his palm. He pressed his forehead to hers and they sat there for a long moment. A strangely spiritual peace filled her.

Rieggar moved just enough to press a kiss against the crown of her head. "When you come, say my name." Then he pulled her to him, and his lips descended into a punishing kiss. She clung to him, breathless and wanting. She opened for his tongue to explore her mouth. No man had kissed her like this before. Her body reacted, and instinctively her tongue found his. He smothered her moans with his fervent kiss until her yearning erupted in flames.

Releasing her roughly, Rieggar put his mouth over her nipple, sucking hard. His hand slipped between her legs, strumming her clit. She bucked under him, writhing with the force of her lust.

"Before we land, I'll hear you scream I own you." Rieggar moved so quickly she had no time to think as he pinned her hands above her head. She lay trapped under his body, his erection pressed into her hip. "Giving your heart to me wouldn't be so bad, would it?"

Her heart thundered. Rieggar held her wrists with one of his large hands while the other ran lightly down her torso. His gaze burned with an intensity that stole her breath. Heat rushed up her neck to blossom in her cheeks.

He continued to hold her in place. Kiijan managed a half-hearted struggle until he spread her legs with his knee. The momentary feeling of violation rekindled her desire even as it brought a flash of panic to the surface of her emotions. Being helpless under him made her struggle for real.

Rieggar moved between her legs, holding her so that he could look down into her eyes. "I will not hurt you. Submit to me."

He was asking too much. She tried to tug free, but he was much stronger.

"Submit," he demanded. "I will release you when you are still. Remain as you are, and lock your fingers."

She stilled, but he didn't let go. They stared at each other for a moment. She tugged, just a little, and his grip tightened. Something uncoiled inside of her and her pussy ached with need. Having him control her was something she'd never had thought she'd like, but she did. She didn't want him to stop. Biting her lip, she locked her fingers and held perfectly still.

They never broke eye contact. He grinned and brushed a gentle kiss against her lips as he released her hands and snuggled his head between her spread thighs. He licked her inner thigh. The strangeness melted away, and her body came alive with sensation. When his hands reached up to play with her sensitive nipples the combination of pleasures coiled desire in her core. A moan slipped from her lips. "Mmm, yes."

Rieggar's mouth worked tirelessly between her spread legs until she was thrashing. He paused his ardent caress. "I will give you what you need, but Kiijan, I need to know you're mine." Rieggar flicked her clit with his tongue and nipping the tender nub. Ever sensation pushed her even closer to the edge. She'd come so many times, but she knew there was something more, something he was holding back.

She bucked. "Please, Rieggar." She ground against him and rubbed her wet pussy against his chin, crying out in frustration.

"Say the words," Rieggar ordered, pinching her nipples, hard. She gasped and arched her back. He cupped her breasts, and his caresses turned tender.

"I give in. Whatever you want."

"That's not what I want." Rieggar kissed her neck until her pussy convulsed, and she groaned with pleasure.

"I'm yours," she panted. Rieggar fucked her with his long fingers while his thumb rolled against her clit. She arched her back and cried out. "I'm so close." She jerked, but never gave up his control. Her fingers remained locked tight. Kiijan pressed her thighs gently against his head. "I -- I need more," she gasped. She moaned and arched her back. "I want... inside... me... please!" Kiijan cried out.

He pulled her up so her knees were on his hips and her legs were wide for him. "And now we become one," he said as his cock found her ready entrance. She gasped with surprise and squeezed her eyes shut as he slipped inside of her with a single thrust and pleasured grunt. There was almost no pain, he entered her so swiftly. The sting burned for a moment, yet the perfect fullness made the discomfort worthwhile. Her tension elevated.

He stilled, his body joined with hers. "It will be good again soon."

Rieggar found her clit, and he strummed her desire back to life. She closed her eyes and let herself stop thinking. Her hands found his ass, and she squeezed his perfection. He began moving inside of her. Carefully, at first, and then with more force. He fit his fingers between them and managed to strum her clit even as he drove hard. She gasped, opening her eyes as she came.

"Rieggar," she cried, their bodies locked together, and her ecstasy began again.

"I love you Kiijan, I swear to you. Soul Unity. With you. I can't understand... how this happened," he panted. His expression appeared strained.

He moved in her again, throwing his head back. His face was taunt. Orgasm rippled through her body, mind, and spirit. Her eyes fluttered closed again as a kaleidoscope of color exploded behind her eyelids. Kiijan shook with the force of her release. This was so much more than the others. Her body responded to him without her conscious decision. She rocked against him, sliding him deeper inside of her. The beautiful friction caused intense tiny little wails of joy to erupt from her throat unhindered.

Kiijan squeezed her eyes closed and just let her body become mindless sensation. Every single stroke of his cock brought a fresh spasm of pleasure through her. He was thrusting hard and fast, and he stroked her clit with his every move. The only sound escaping her were little whimpers of pleasure. Kiijan opened her eyes and gazed at Rieggar. His face twisted into a mask of concentration as he pumped inside of her, and she arched her back as Rieggar drove deeper. The pleasure didn't ebb. The physical joy continued as the seconds became timeless. Nothing mattered but this man and his cock. A keening wail left her throat, and her breath hitched. Nothing in her whole experience prepared her for this nirvana.

"You feel amazing," he muttered through his gritted teeth.

Carnality splintered through her, and she arched off his mattress. He stopped when he was deep inside her. Her pussy contracted instantly as her sensitivity peaked. She gripped him with her inner muscles as he thrust into her a final time. The heat of his seed filled her. He held her, and they shook from the intensity -- pleasure so great it grew into something akin to pain. The sensation was so overwhelming her eyes watered.

"You were made for me," he whispered.

She wept, hard, sobbing with the uncontrollable expression of emotion. Rieggar held her and pushed the hair off her face. The smell of sex perfumed the air. He turned her head to the side, facing him, and smiled at her before placing a kiss to her mouth. He didn't let her pull away as he tugged her closer. They fit together perfectly. His body heat seeped into her soul. Her mind floated disconnectedly as her body indulged in the afterglow of mating.

* * *

Kiijan couldn't make eye contact with her aunt. Aunt Sofia paced in her luxury apartment. "Your mother is going to kill me. Your fathers, too. What were you thinking? Married? Without permission?"

"I thought you'd understand."

"I do, but your parents won't. How could you be so cruel to them? Your mother loves you so much. You should be ashamed."

"I'm not. I'm in love." She wasn't lying. When she'd woken in Rieggar's arms, she'd realized she didn't want to stay on Earth. She'd never understood how women let men control them until the moment he'd woken and told her to get ready to see her aunt. She hadn't even realized he'd ordered her until she was clean and dressed. She'd discovered that during the night Rieggar had gotten up and washed her clothing before returning to bed.

"You know Mom will be happy if I'm happy."

Her aunt's face softened. "She will. Your mother is the best person I've ever known. But you've put her in a tough spot. She'll have to intercede between your fathers and your husband. I sent them your message."

As if on cue, her interplanetary comm blinked and chirped from the coffee table. It was time to face the music.

"Sis? Yeah, she's right here." Aunt Sofia motioned her over.

Kiijan leaned over the comm. "Hi, Mom."

Her mother's face was tear-stained, and the sight kindled her guilt. "Are you okay?"

"Yes."

"Thank the Mother. Did he... hurt you?"

"No Mom. Rieggar is wonderful. I -- I'm in love with him."

Her mother's expression softened. "Well, if he's convinced you to love him he must be an amazing man."

Heat filled Kiijan's face as memories of the previous night filled her mind. "He is. I think Dads know him."

"They do, and they are not happy at all. He caused a lot of dissension when he was younger. You know he was a warrior, right? They just don't understand why he was better than the warrior they picked for you."

"Don't. Seriously, we're Soul Bonded. Please tell them that."

"They saw the same message I saw, and they don't care. They'll always think they know best. I'm sure your Rieggar understands this is not going to be an easy welcome home, but please come home. Don't stay on Earth."

"I can't. Where Rieggar is, I am home."

Her mother smiled. "I understand. I was once in the same situation of a surprising bond. I wanted my freedom too and then *bam*, nothing mattered to me but how much I loved my husbands. They are outraged he won't consider a second."

"I know, but I don't want anything to do with a Soul Trinity. We're not at war anymore. They need to get with the times."

Alexa rolled her eyes. "And you need to respect your fathers. Politically, Xerra has never been stable. War could find you, and your Rieggar, unprepared."

"I love all of you. I respect you, but you don't respect me. That's why I had to run."

Her mother leaned closer to the comm and lowered her voice. "Why didn't you tell us? If you'd fallen in love with someone why didn't you just tell them when they announced you were to marry. I know they have -- issues -- with your husband's choices, but they'd have been very happy you found a warrior without them. Even one who'd left the brotherhood is better than a man they'd see as inferior. I..." Her eyes welled with tears. "I wasn't able to see you married."

"Rieggar is a good man. He recorded our ceremony without telling me. You'll get to see it."

Her mother wiped her eyes with handkerchief. "That's better than nothing, I guess. Tell him thank you. I want him to be comfortable with us so he'll bring you home to me -- often. And your children. Oh, children. I'm so hopeful! Your brothers are taking far too long. You are planning to start a family, aren't you?"

Kiijan ducked her head so her mother wouldn't see the smile. "Mom!"

"Don't make me wait too long."

Aunt Sofia laughed. "She's been complaining about grandchildren to me for so long that I'd suggest you have a baby immediately. Sis, if it makes you feel any better, I just want you to know I've seen the way he looks at her. He loves her."

Alexa appeared relieved. "I'll play interference with your fathers if you promise to come home as soon as he's done with his business. And bring me some chocolate."

"I will. I need to get going. My husband's delivery should be dropped off by now. I'm going to show him around the city, and then we're going to eat at the Earthiest place I know, McDonalds."

"That might kill him."

"He's stronger than you'd think. He's willing to marry the daughter of two warriors without permission. There's also the matter of my bridal funds. I want to stay with him and live on the *Revolution* -- his ship. I thought I wanted freedom, but I'm afraid my soul is enslaved."

"Stupid and strong are not the same thing. Don't you look at me like that. I'm kidding. I love you. I can't believe any male has won your heart. He is worthy, or he wouldn't have you. I'll make sure your fathers do what's right and release the money to you and your Rieggar. Just make sure he knows if he hurts you it won't be your fathers he should fear."

Kiijan chuckled. Her mother was skilled with

weapons, both of her fathers had seen to that. Rieggar had no idea how dangerous loving her was. She shook her head, but her smile widened. "I will make sure he knows."

Her mother's eyes misted. "I miss you. Give your aunt the biggest hug for me. Safe travels."

The comm disconnected. Kiijan turned to look at her aunt. "I might have found my freedom isn't exactly what I thought it would be, but that doesn't mean I'll stop believing my people can change."

Aunt Sofia's eyes misted as she nodded. The unspoken ghost of Alexa's sacrifice hung between them.

Kiijan's brows drew together. "I'll never stop fighting for the other women on my world. Not all of them are happy with how things are. The truest definition of choice is having the right to make one."

A knock made them both turn to the door and dispelled the sadness permeating the room. Aunt Sofia went over and looked at the external video monitor next to the door. She turned to Kiijan and grinned. Without saying anything she opened the door.

Rieggar stood next to Ellar, waiting. When he saw Kiijan there was a change in his face, and she saw his love for her. He enthralled her, and she gazed back at him lost in the intensity between them.

Ellar broke the spell by kissing Aunt Sofia's hand. "You must be the most beautiful treasure on Earth," he uttered with reverence.

His words inspired a far too girlish giggle from her aunt. Kiijan hid her grin behind her hand.

Rieggar glared at his friend. "This woman is my family now. Respect her."

Ellar's hot gaze raked over Sofia. "Of course."

Kiijan was having trouble keeping the laughter

inside and covered with a cough. Rieggar turned to her in alarm. "Are you well? Is this planet causing you distress?"

She rolled her eyes. "I'm fine."

Rieggar's expression relaxed, but there was still a shadow of worry in his gaze. "I am having a great deal of trouble with this whole freedom issue. I want to pick you up and carry you to the ship where I can keep you safe."

She glared at her husband. "But you won't." She couldn't keep the challenge out of her tone.

He sighed. "I won't. It might destroy me, but I will never force my will on you. My soul has touched yours, and I know your needs. I will always put your joy before my own."

His words chased away her fears. "I love you."

Tenderness took over his features as he crossed the room to take her in his arms. "I thought it was money I needed, but I was wrong."

She gazed up into his eyes. "You were?"

"Yes." Rieggar kissed the tip of her nose. "I needed you."

"And you have me." She kissed his chin. "But I have my bridal money and we'll be able to pay off the debts and finish the repairs to *Revolution*. Besides, we'll need to make it child safe."

A look of wonder filled him.

"Yes. Your seed lives within me."

He dropped to his knees before her, wrapping his arms around her middle, and kissed her stomach. Then, he rested his forehead against her midsection. "I-I'm overwhelmed by the gift you are to me." His tone sounded choked. "Thank you, my princess, you have given me a kingdom of treasures and I have nothing to give you."

"I only need one thing."

"Name it and I shall see you have it."

"Silly male." She kissed the top of his head, stroking his long hair. "Your heart."

"It's yours for the rest of my existence."

And it was…

Ashlynn Monroe

Ashlynn Monroe is a busy working mom. She loves her kids and family. Her greatest joy is creating stories to entertain others, and she hopes they bring a little more romance into the world. She's been writing since her teens for her own enjoyment but decided in her thirties to share her imagination with readers. Ashlynn enjoys biking, camping, reading, video games, and filling her home and life with love. If she's not working or chasing children, you can find her daydreaming up her next tale of romance.

More books by Ashlynn Monroe: changelingpress.com/ashlynn-monroe-a-166

Changeling Press E-Books

More Sci-Fi, Fantasy, Paranormal, and BDSM adventures available in e-book format for immediate download at ChangelingPress.com -- Werewolves, Vampires, Dragons, Shapeshifters and more -- Erotic Tales from the edge of your imagination.

What are E-Books?

E-books, or electronic books, are books designed to be read in digital format -- on your desktop or laptop computer, notebook, tablet, Smart Phone, or any electronic e-book reader.

Where can I get Changeling Press E-Books?

Changeling Press e-books are available at ChangelingPress.com, Amazon, Apple Books, Barnes & Noble, and Kobo/Walmart.

Changeling Press, LLC

ChangelingPress.com